Sundered

BOOK ONE OF THE NEVERMORE TRILOGY

Sundered (The Nevermore Trilogy, Book 1) Anniversary Edition

Copyright © Shannon Mayer 2016
Copyright © HiJinks Ink Publishing, Ltd. 2016
All rights reserved

Published by HiJinks Ink LTD.
www.shannonmayer.com

Original Cover Art by Damon Za
Mayer, Shannon

Sundered

BOOK ONE OF THE NEVERMORE TRILOGY

SHANNON
MAYER

Also By Shannon Mayer

The Rylee Adamson Novels

Priceless (Book 1)
Immune (Book 2)
Raising Innocence (Book 3)
Shadowed Threads (Book 4)
Blind Salvage (Book 5)
Tracker (Book 6)
Veiled Threat (Book 7)
Wounded (Book 8)
Rising Darkness (Book 9)
Blood of the Lost (Book 10)
Alex (A Short Story)
Tracking Magic (A Novella 0.25)
Elementally Priceless (A Novella 0.5)
Guardian (A Novella 6.5)
Stitched (A Novella 8.5)

The Rylee Adamson Epilogues

RYLEE (Book 1)
LIAM (Book 2)
PAMELA (Book 3)

A Celtic Legacy

Dark Waters (Book 1)
Dark Isle (Book 2)
Dark Fae (Book 3)

The Risk Series
(Written as S.J. Mayer)

High Risk Love (Book 1)

Contemporary Romances
(Written as S.J. Mayer)

Of The Heart

SUNDERED

Love is something eternal; the aspect may change, but not the essence.

-Vincent Van Gogh

CHAPTER ONE

Mara

I walked slowly, my hands above my head as if I were a prisoner being marched to her death. All to keep from touching the wild weeds around me. Brilliantly yellow with tiny little flowers that so many people thought were pretty, the Scotch broom seemed to reach for me. Me. The one so damn allergic to the stuff that just looking at it set my nose to itching. One branch dipped my way. "Don't you dare." I glared at it as if that would stop it from brushing against me. I ducked under the cursed thing and hurried forward.

Here I was, walking in a veritable Death Valley of flora. It rose around me, far above my head and crushed in from both sides. My eyes watered, my throat and nose itched with every breath I took, and the patches of bare skin the plant had already leaned in to kiss were bright red and swelling into a scattering of hives.

Fanny Bay, on the eastern side of Vancouver Island, was famous for a lot of things—oysters and eclectic artisans at the top of that list. But when we moved to the small town three months ago, I didn't realize it was a breeding ground for my most hated nemesis. That's what we got for checking it out in winter.

"You coming, babe? I really am sorry; I didn't know the trail was full of this stuff." Sebastian, my sweet and usually thoughtful husband, yelled back to me. He wasn't allergic to the spazzy yellow plant, so he didn't have to worry about the branches that hung on all sides. Because of that, he made good time on the trail and was swiftly leaving me behind. I could just make out his broad back and dark brown hair over the tops of the Broom stalks ahead of me. At 6'4", he towered over most people and living things, noxious weeds included.

"Yeah, right." I grunted my reply, not wanting to take in any more air than I had to. The walk through the tunnel of broom wouldn't kill me—it wasn't that bad of an allergy—but hell, it wasn't something I enjoyed dealing with either. Breaking out in a rash and blowing my nose continually in between fits of sneezing for the next few hours was what I had to look forward to after this little daytrip.

Bottom line was, even I needed to get out into the fresh air. I'd been holed up far too long grieving a loss I could do nothing about. Our little hike and visit with the new neighbors would get me moving. God love the man, sometimes Sebastian knew me better than I knew myself. The excursion had been his idea, a last ditch attempt to draw me out of the depression that had me in its grip.

"Mara?"

"I'm coming, Bastian. Don't expect me to run through this crap." I shifted sideways to slip between two overhanging branches.

A broken off, half-dead tree jabbed me in the belly with a wayward branch, and I snapped it off with a quick twist. "Stupid plant."

Of all the things that had been jabbed into me of late: needles, pills, advice . . . the tree was the least painful, both to my body and heart.

I blinked away tears that suddenly threatened, and wiped my hands across my eyes, brushing the traitorous emotion away. All to my immediate regret: my hands were covered in pollen from pushing the broom out of my way.

"Son of a donkey's ass, I'm an idiot," I muttered as I blinked furiously, doing my best to keep the tears flowing in a vain effort to rinse my eyes.

I couldn't seem to escape my most recent past. No matter what I did these days, there was always something to remind me how broken I was. The doctors didn't know why we were having such a hard time not only getting pregnant, but carrying a child to term. The latest miscarriage made me feel like it was my fault. As if a perfect confirmation that it was my body that refused to hang onto a child, that there was something intrinsically wrong with me. Of course, no one said it out loud. Maybe the fear was all in my head. At least that's what one of the doctors had said when we were in the hospital, and he'd been taking what was left of our baby from me.

My throat tightened and it had nothing to do with the plants around me causing a reaction. I couldn't stop my mind from spinning backward through all the things we'd tried to help us get pregnant. Reiki. Acupuncture. Weight loss. Vitamins. Detoxes. Fertility medicine. Anything I could find on the internet I tried in desperation. The cost of fertility pills wasn't much, and they were what allowed us to even get pregnant the last two times.

When we finally looked into IVF the cost . . .well the cost of in vitro fertilization was close to fifteen thousand dollars. And that's if it worked the first time around and we didn't need to use it again, and again. Not to mention we had nothing left in our savings account after buying the house. If I'd known we would have to be looking at IVF, I wouldn't have agreed to the move at all. We could always buy a house in the future. There were only so many years that I could potentially have a child.

Maybe we just weren't meant to have a baby, maybe there was something wrong with us that—I sneezed again and rubbed my nose with the back of my hand. The minor explosion jarred me out of my thoughts.

"Hurry up, woman. I told Dan we'd be there ten minutes ago. Last thing I want is to upset the neighbors." Sebastian's voice was even farther ahead now. Wonderful. Just what I wanted, to rush through the broom, taking even more blows to my sensitive skin, eyes, and nose.

"Yeah, I'm coming, O white knight of mine who considers a walk in the broom a nice time out for his highly allergic wife!" I yelled back.

I wasn't angry with him, not really. This was part of the way he dealt with his own grief. It was the same when his father and brother died in the boating accident; at least, that was what his mother shared with me the night before on the phone.

"Mara, he didn't know how to handle the pain. So he just buckled down and moved on. Bastian is all about pushing forward and not looking behind. Honey, he's trying to help you in his own way, if you'll let him." She sighed softly. "I'm sorry. I wish you two didn't have these troubles. Don't worry, there will be more babies."

I'd hung up on her at that point. Why was it people thought having more babies made the loss of this one any less? No, I wasn't about to go there. Not today.

I shook my head and deliberately took my thoughts back to Sebastian. Even with his push forward and don't look back motto, he'd sweated the whole way across the Georgia Strait. The main transport on or off Vancouver Island was the BC Ferries. It didn't seem to matter to Bastian that the ferry was literally the size of a cruise liner and you couldn't feel the waves. He'd sat in one place, folded his arms, and kept his eyes shut the entire hour and a half crossing. And driving off the boat once we'd docked? You'd think he'd been a part of NASCAR.

He didn't like boats, didn't like water, and didn't make any bones about it.

A crack of twigs within the bush stopped my feet.

"Sebastian?" He had a nasty habit of scaring me, jumping out from the place I least expected. The rustling drew closer and I pulled away, pressing my back against a wall of yellow and green, my heart picking up speed. Even though he did it to me all the time, I still jumped.

But this time. . .I didn't think it was Sebastian. A musky odor floated past my nose, and whatever it was hiding behind the thick plants was an animal. There was a flash of black in the bush across from me and I let out a tiny squeak and then clamped my hands over my mouth.

Black bears were more than common on this part of Vancouver Island; they were considered part of the neighborhood and one of the few things I was truly terrified of. They could be huge, too. There was plenty of food in the area, with excessive amounts of fish and berries at the tip of their paws. That being said, it didn't make them any less dangerous because they weren't as hungry as bears in other parts.

Crap, maybe I was just. . .smelling things? I mean, I could barely smell past the snot running. So maybe that was it. Mouth dry, I tried again, cleared my throat and whispered as loud as I dared. "Sebastian!"

The black thing in the bush that I was now pretty damn sure was a bear, grunted and shuffled closer, and I slid my way toward the spot where I'd last seen my husband. The branches and twigs snapped as it moved, pushing its way through. Maybe the bear wouldn't attack us if we were together. Was there safety in numbers with a bear? I wasn't sure. But I didn't want to die alone.

Sweat popped out on my forehead and I no longer cared how much the broom brushed me, I didn't want to be eaten. I pushed my back against the wall of plants, not caring that they scratched across my bare skin as I slid sideways up the trail keeping my eyes trained on the rustling bush behind me.

One more step forward and something grabbed me from behind sending me into a flailing mass of arms, legs, and terrified squeaks as my heart threatened to burst out of my throat.

"Whoa, whoa, babe, settle down." Sebastian laughed at me, his blue eyes dancing, his hands resting on my shoulders.

I didn't care that he'd scared me. Not this time. I gulped in a breath and spluttered a single word. "Bear." I pointed down the trail where I'd been only moments before, my hand shaking so hard it looked like I was having a seizure.

His eyebrows shot up and he looked over my head. "Really? Are you sure?"

I nodded. "Yes. I could smell it."

Then the stupidest thing I've ever seen that man of mine do happened right in front of my disbelieving eyes.

Sebastian started back the way we'd come, toward the bear.

"What are you doing?" I whispered, my fear turning to anger as I thought of myself widowed before I'd even turned thirty.

"I just want to see it. I've never seen a bear up close before," he said. As if that made all the sense in the world.

"There's a first and a last time for everything," I snapped. But then contrite at the thought of my last words to him being snotty, I changed tactics. "Please come back, we need to keep going. I thought you said we were almost there." I couldn't help but scratch at one of my arms, the itching not going away even with all the adrenaline. If anything, I think it made it worse.

Sebastian didn't answer me except to wave backwards casually. Like he needed me to stay back. As if I was going to get any closer to the bear. One of us had to keep our head screwed on straight.

He kept moving forward, his movements slow and steady as if he was afraid to spook the animal. Somehow, I didn't think that was going to be a problem.

I wanted to scrub my hands over my face with frustration, but at the last minute recalled the amount of broom I'd been touching, and had to settle for gripping the edges of my shorts. There had to be a way to get him to come back.

"Sebastian, I'll divorce you if you keep looking for the bear."

"You're too poor to pay a lawyer," he said.

I snorted. "So are you." I thought a moment more, then knew I had the answer. "I'll tell your Gran on you."

He stopped, stood up straight and turned to face me. "You wouldn't."

The look on his face said it all and a twitch started in the corner of my lips. I had him now. I let out a sigh of relief and put my hands on my hips.

"I would, just you wait and—"

A huge black bear burst out of the bush behind Sebastian with a roar. I bit down on a scream as my worst nightmare unfolded before my eyes. Sebastian stumbled back in my direction, and fell over a bulging root in the ground. I grabbed a rock, cocked my arm to throw it, then a hand dropped on my shoulder and shoved me to the ground none too gently. The smell of cigar smoke curled through the air, slicing through the sweet musk of the broom and the heavier musk of the large predator that was ready to eat my husband.

"Stay down, girl," a throaty voice said and I looked over my shoulder to see one of our neighbors above me with a gun leveled at the bear. "You too, boy, stay down."

I wasn't sure if he was talking to Sebastian or the bear.

We both stayed low and the neighbor, I thought his name was Dan, walked toward the big animal, his gun never wavering. The bear stayed on his back legs, standing tall, easily taller than Sebastian. My mouth was dry, and I couldn't stop the shaking in my muscles as I lay there, hoping the gun went off.

"Come on, Bob. You know you aren't allowed to be eatin' the locals. Specially these city folk that are so new here. You know, they're practically a biohazard with all the toxins and chemicals they've been living in. Full of shit you don't want to eat."

"Hey, we eat healthy," I muttered, then thought about the situation and shut my mouth. We were caught between an obviously crazy man holding a loaded gun and a bear in the middle of a forested trail no one knew we were on.

Be quiet, Mara. You'll live longer.

I watched in disbelief as the bear—Bob, I guess—dropped to all fours and let out a long low snort which ended up spraying snot in all directions. He shook his big head hard side to side like he was not impressed with the situation. The bear's reaction was all too human for me.

"Yeah," Dan said, "I feel the same about these imports, but we got to give them a chance before we run them off. Maybe they'll be good for something, hey?"

The bear grunted and pawed at the ground a mere foot away from Sebastian's bare legs. I whimpered in fear, wishing I had the gun in my hands. Why wasn't Dan shooting the bear? He wasn't truly having a conversation with the animal; he had to know that, didn't he?

Or was he as crazy as the other neighbors said?

"Go on now, Bob. Come around back of the house later tonight and you can have one of the salmon I thawed out this morning," Dan said as he lowered the gun. Bob gave one last snuffle, grunted, and turned away. His big black bum wobbled side to side as he wandered back into the bush, heading toward the ocean.

I scrambled to my feet and ran to Sebastian, catching him in a, dare I say it, bear hug.

"I'm okay, babe," he said into my hair.

"No, you're not." I let him go and kicked him in the shin, pleased with the wince it produced. "You idiot! I told you not to go back and look, but you couldn't listen, could you? That bear could have killed you!"

"Lower your voice, girl, or Bob will come back to see what all the shouting's about, and to be honest, I'd sooner shoot you than him. He's better company than most people," Dan said.

I turned to face him, our kind-of rescuer, at a loss for words. Did I say thanks for saving us, or thanks for not shooting us, or was I supposed to be mad that he preferred a bear over people? Dan stared at me as he chewed on the stubby cigar clamped between yellowed teeth. His salt and pepper hair was close to military short and yet still managed to be messy with a number of strands that were far too long. Like they'd been missed by the hair clippers. He wore rumpled and stained army fatigues and boots that were well scuffed. I didn't know what to make of him. Was it an act, or were the other locals right and he was off his rocker?

Sebastian took the lead, exaggerating his limp and

rubbing at his shin before holding his hand out to the gruff older man. "Thanks, Dan, we much appreciate the intervention with your friend there. We were on our way to your place. You put an ad on the mailbox that said you had some old gardening stuff you want to get rid of. I spoke with you this morning about coming by."

Dan stared at Sebastian for so long, I started to get nervous. The man after all had a reputation for eating Crazy Flakes for breakfast and he was packing a large gun. Not really a good combination in any situation. I cleared my throat.

"I think the paper said you had things like old pots, and maybe even some veggie starts," I said, wanting to break the awkward silence.

Dan took a drag on his cigar and blew out a string of smoke. "Yup, come on then." He turned his back to us, put his gun over his shoulder and led us down the yellow and green tunnel. Suddenly the plants were the least of my worries.

We followed, Sebastian taking my hand and giving it a squeeze. "I'm sorry," he mouthed to me.

I smiled and squeezed his hand. "Okay. But I'm still calling your Gran."

Sebastian winced again and I nodded. There was always a consequence for being dumb, even if it was just having your Gran rip a strip off you.

As the adrenaline stopped its headlong rush through my body, I became acutely aware of my bare legs and arms—all the parts I'd shoved against the broom. By the time we reached Dan's place, every visible inch of me was covered in hives. I stared around, absently scratching at my arms.

The house was a veritable fortress of a home that looked as if it had once been part army barracks, it was so buttoned up. The yard wasn't fenced, but it didn't need to be, not with the way the house was built. What looked like steel plate covered the doors, and all the windows had rebar grills over them. To be fair though, there weren't many windows even on the lower levels. I could only see two from where I stood. The entire exterior of the house seemed to be made of a cement brick mixture. I ran my fingers over the rough texture, my curiosity for a moment overwhelming my itching. Yes, cement. The house was built of cement. I shivered. I would not want to live in a place that was so . . .cold. It would be like living in a tomb.

I made my way to Sebastian, touching him on the arm. "Please make this quick, Bastian. I'm blowing up like a puffer fish, here."

"Will do." He kissed me on the forehead, his attention already back on the plant starters at his feet.

I took a few steps back and deposited myself on the only chair in the yard. Rickety and obviously well used, I waited for it to fold up on me like a Venus Fly Trap. When it held me, I let out sigh of relief.

Dan strolled over to my side, and deposited a prickly cactus looking plant on the ground beside me.

"What's that?" I stared at it. Surely that wasn't one of the veggie starts? It looked . . .odd.

He grunted. "Aloe Vera. It'll help with the rash until you get home." He broke off a thick green stem and handed the goopy end to me. I took it, lifted my eyebrow at him and he motioned for me to rub it on the hives. With my eyebrows high and my nose wrinkled, I did as he said.

The burning itch subsided a little within seconds. "Oh, that is nice. Thank you." He was already walking away from me though, and I wasn't sure he even heard me.

Surprised at his kindness, my opinion of him shifted again. Maybe he wasn't the weird old man people said he was. I broke off a second piece of the plant and rubbed it onto the worst patch of hives with a sigh. It was cool and soothing. I needed to get myself an Aloe Vera plant.

Where I sat in the shade, I had to admit the view wasn't bad if I didn't look at the blocky square of the house. This corner of Dan's garden was already showing some bright green sprouts up through the dark earth even though it was early May. I recognized a few—the peas, I'll admit it was mostly the peas. I was still rather new to the whole concept of gardening anything other than a few flowers in the windowsill in a high-rise apartment. We'd lived in Edmonton for years and had pretty much stayed indoors because of the excessive heat and bugs in the summer, and the brutally cold winters. Which didn't leave me excited about being outside in general.

I could see what I thought were maybe beans next to the peas climbing a section of netting, along with some large rubber tires that housed several tiny plants that could have been lettuce starts. Next to that were several raised beds with strawberries. Those at least I could pick out easily. A huge compost pile was in the back and all sorts of things sprouted from that. Like the leftovers of all the seeds in the world had just taken hold and went wild in the poo pile.

I snorted softly to myself.

The mixture of old-school gardening life next to the military feel of his home was odd to say the least.

On the doorstep leading into the house, a battered old radio played while Sebastian talked planting, tools, and seeds with Dan. The low hum of their voices and the slowing of my heart allowed me to close my eyes.

Peace, if fleeting, was something I desperately missed the last few months. I put a hand to my belly, wishing it had continued to swell. Wondering if I ever would . . . no. This was not the time or place to think about that.

Fifteen minutes into the visit, Dan turned the radio up. "Local news is on. Heard there is some big stuff happening."

A female announcer came on, her voice breathy and completely unsuited to radio. I cringed, thinking she would be better off doing phone sex.

"Bet she got the job by doing a few jobs of her own, eh?" Dan gave me a lecherous wink and walked over to where Sebastian was digging through an old pile of pots.

I grimaced and shook my head, partly because my own mind had gone in that same direction. No matter that it was probably true. I reached down to rub at a particularly large hive on the back of my calf with a piece of the Aloe Vera.

The announcers voice suddenly pitched even higher and I blinked several times when I caught the gist of what she was saying. This was the local news, and I knew the talent pool was small, but still, the announcer was terrible. I mean . . . really, really bad.

"This is a miracle drug, boys and girls. Not only can you eat whatever you want and not gain weight, but it does all sorts of great things. You can't buy it over the counter. This is a shot. So a yucky needle, but so worth it. . ."

I got up and moved my chair closer to the radio as a second announcer came on. His voice was highly animated and almost as feminine as the woman's. In fact, it was difficult to tell who was who.

"So, Phillipa, you're telling me there's no downside, no side effects to this—what was the drug called again?" he asked.

Phillipa's irritating voice came back on. "They're calling it Nevermore, as in, never more gain weight, never more get sick, or disgustingly fat, never more get cellulite, or any sort of weight gain." She giggled and the high pitch and redundancy of what she was saying made me shiver. It was a wonder the speakers didn't blow out. She took an audibly deep breath and continued, "It's amazing, one shot is all it takes, and yes, it is expensive, but that's it. Five thousand dollars and one shot and you're good for life. I've lost ten pounds, and I've been eating burgers, cake, and totally noshing on chocolate."

The male announcer came back on.

"Reportedly, this Nevermore truly is a miracle drug as it also prevents Parkinson's disease, works in tandem with heart medications to stop arrhythmias, and has a host of other beneficial side effects. One that will be of interest to many is that it helps tremendously with fertility, more so than any of the current fertility drugs, with less side effects and downsides. As it's derived from an all-natural source, the body can utilize it in a way other drugs don't mesh . . ."

I turned the radio down and looked over to Sebastian talking away at Dan. But Dan was looking at me. He'd heard the announcers, too, and the look in his eyes was not good. They were narrowed, deep lines around the edges and his mouth was pinched with worry.

He locked eyes with me. "That ain't going to lead to anything good. You mark my words."

Bastian startled. "What? I thought that the potatoes had to go in that deep."

I turned from Dan's gaze so I could watch them out of the corner of my eye.

Dan had gone back to speaking with my husband. Every once in a while, Dan nodded, but he didn't smile, not even once. But it was Bastian who I kept looking back to. He was not only tall, but a little on the large side. Okay, a little more than a little on the large side. Not that I had anything to preen about, I easily had an extra twenty-five pounds on my 5'5" frame. Maybe even thirty, but it was still less than I'd been carrying a year ago when we decided to start our family. That was when we realized there was a problem and might not be able to have a baby. I lost weight, ate healthy, took my pre-natal vitamins, but getting pregnant was nearly impossible and the two times I did, I miscarried.

The things the announcers had talked about though . . . was it possible?

Scratching at my collarbone, I had a sudden urge to get moving. Not only did I need to get a double dose of antihistamines and a shower to wash the broom pollen off, I had to get on the phone to the doctor about this. What if this Nevermore drug was what the radio said it was? It seemed almost too good to be true: fertility and weight loss, all rolled into a single shot. Adoption could take years of waiting. Surrogacy was as expensive as IVF. For five thousand dollars we could have our own child. I could finally feel a child grow within my belly. I was sure we could pull five thousand off the line of credit. We had a home now, which would make good collateral.

My heart started to thrum with excitement. This was what we'd been waiting for. I could hardly wait to tell Sebastian what I'd heard; I could hardly wait to finally be a mother and start our life as a family.

Chapter Two

Sebastian

Mara thought I hadn't heard what the announcer said. All the way home, though, she told me about it. Several times.

I didn't want to burst her bubble. She was too happy. And it had been so long since I'd seen her smile like this, like her world was beautiful again. So I smiled back, and held her hand tightly, and did my best to push back the desire to tell her it wouldn't work.

The latest miscarriage had been harder on her than I thought. Stupidly, I thought after the first one, that a second wouldn't be that big of a deal. I was wrong, of course.

In the middle of packing boxes for our move, she'd suddenly doubled over in pain, clutching at her belly. The look on her face stayed with me even now. She'd known, and the grief and fear that had etched itself in her eyes . . . I wasn't sure I'd ever be able to erase it.

Though we'd rushed her to the hospital, there had been nothing the doctors could do.

I swallowed hard, thinking of the long night in the hospital, holding her hand. She'd been given a heavy sedative, and hadn't realized she'd lost the baby. A night where I held onto her, wishing I would not have to be the one to tell her.

A sigh slipped out of me as we reached our little house.

"You okay? Aren't you excited about this?" Mara tugged on my hand, all but dragging me to the house.

I laughed. "Sure, what are we excited about again?"

"Stop teasing me!" She laughed with me and her blue eyes danced with happiness. Happy, she was *so* happy. I didn't want to take that from her. I'd hoped that in moving to the island, she would find some peace, that maybe we could try again for a baby. But I agreed with Dan . . . a drug that did so much, what would the negative side effects be? Did those who created it even know? Why couldn't she wait a little bit and make sure it was as good as they said? I sure as hell didn't want to be a pin cushion guinea pig.

Stopping at the edge of the back porch, I stared at the home in front of me. Our little farmhouse wasn't much, but it was ours. And one day, it would be filled with laughter and the patter of little feet, of that much I was sure. Or, at least, I hoped I was sure. Mara let my hand go and bolted into the house, shedding clothes as she ran.

I grinned as she wiggled out of her shorts and then disappeared through the back door. I made my way up onto the porch and looked around the property, as far as I could see. Five acres, and most of it had been cleared, which meant we could have chickens for eggs, or a milk cow or something useful like that. I grimaced. What was I thinking? I did not want to be waking up to some stupid rooster crowing its head off, and knowing my luck, I'd end up with a yard full of roosters instead of hens. Cows then. Maybe we could stick to cows.

The house was old, easily a hundred years according to the real estate agent who helped us find it. Part of the reason we'd been able to afford it on our meagre incomes was that it was a real fixer upper. From the fence surrounding the place that we'd redone completely, to the gardens, to the old barn out back, and of course, the house itself, everything needed help.

I scrubbed a hand through my hair and let out a breath. The walk to and from Dan's had winded me. I sat on the steps of the porch.

"I gotta get in shape," I said out loud even though it was just me. Damn, how many times had I said that? I was almost thirty and I still was trying to lose the weight I'd gained in college. Sweat trickled down my back after the long hike. I glanced at the thermometer hanging on the wall next to the kitchen window. Not even seventy-five degrees and I was sweating. The summer wasn't even fully on us yet.

A snap of cool ocean air curled toward me and I twisted where I sat. This was one of the perks of the place we lived. We had an ocean view even though we weren't right on the water. From our place we had a decent view of the silvery blue expanse, almost one hundred eighty degrees with only a few trees breaking it up. The waves and barking sea lions could be heard most days. I shuddered. The view had been important for Mara, not me.

An image of my brother reaching for my hand as he sunk under the water of the ocean flashed through my mind. I gripped the edge of the stairs and turned sharply from the ocean view. I pushed the memory back, pushed away the panic and grief that came with it.

The sound of the shower coming on in the second-floor bathroom caught my ears. A distraction was what I needed. The present was all that mattered, not the past.

Mara was my present, and my future. I smiled, stood, and jogged into the house and up the stairs.

Chapter Three

Mara

I ran upstairs to shower, hoping to wash all the pollen from my skin. I knew from experience that the water would feel like a little piece of heaven on the hives.

Our home, I was completely in love with it, along with all the history it represented. The rooms were heated with a woodstove that sat in the center of the house, and it even had an old wood-burning cooking stove that was now on the back porch having made room for my new convection oven. The old woman who owned the farmhouse had been on the property her whole life, ninety-eight years, and had not only been raised in the house, but had raised her own children in the house. I'd hoped to raise our children here.

My hands slowed in the soapy water as my thoughts wound back to the hospital, the nurses and the doctor telling me I had miscarried the first time. At five weeks, still in my first trimester and within the real danger zone, I'd woken in the middle of the night to cramping and blood on the sheets. Since then I'd not gone back to my job as a real estate agent, choosing instead to take a leave of absence to deal with the grief and to give my body time to heal.

The second miscarriage . . . it had happened not that much further into the pregnancy. I'd made it to six weeks and had begun to allow myself to hope since I'd made it farther along than the time before.

The look on Sebastian's face when I'd woken in the hospital. His words, so carefully crafted, they had done nothing to ease the pain that had shot through me like a lightning bolt.

The bathroom door clicked and I poked my head outside the curtain. "Hand me the new shampoo, please."

Sebastian held it just out of reach, playing a game of cat and mouse, before finally letting me take it. A grin spread across his face, his gorgeous dimples framing his mouth.

I ducked back in and lathered up, smiling to myself. He might be a little chubby, but my man was good-looking and that smile of his made me weak in the knees. More than one lady had fallen prey to his charms before I came along. I knew that. Even now, he had the local neighborhood ladies all in a tizzy. Every time one of them caught him at the mailbox, he came home with a story about how he'd been told how wonderful he was. And how the older ladies wished their daughters had married someone so sweet and cute as him.

Some of it was bragging, but I had no doubt some of it was truth, too.

I scrubbed the shampoo into my hair, working the lather thoroughly.

"It's probably a hoax, you know that, don't you, babe?" Sebastian's voice was muffled as I stuck my head under the running water. The cool shower sluiced off the last of the pollen. It didn't, however, make the hives go away. I was covered in them from head to toe, the bumps starting to develop even where the plant didn't touch me, its infection of my skin spreading like some horrid disease.

"You don't know that and neither do I," I said, soaping my body up again. Better to be safe than sorry when it came to getting all the pollen off. "You aren't a doctor last time I checked, Bastian. And I'm not going to just run into this. I'll look it up." I wasn't a complete fool.

"These sorts of things come and go. It's either a total con or it will turn out to have some horrible side effect. Like, your boobs will shrivel up leaving me nothing to play with, and then I would die. And you'd be boob-less. The world would be a dark place, my love, if that happened."

I laughed, turned the water off and reached for a towel that hung beside the shower. The curtain slid open and Sebastian lifted an eyebrow at me, a smile tugging at the corner of his lips. His clothes seemed to have mysteriously disappeared. His eyes roved over my naked and still-wet body. Heat curled in my stomach. Even now after four years of marriage, he could set my body on fire and my heart racing with a simple look of desire.

"The towel, please." I held out my hand, doing my best to look uninterested. He shook his head and stepped into the tub, his bare toes touching the tips of mine. Without a word he started to dry me off with the towel. Starting with my hair and working his way slowly down my body, his hands massaging every inch of me as he dried my skin.

I bit back a groan, as the moisture from my skin disappeared and the heat between us intensified. I closed my eyes and let the sensations wash through me.

"Stop, we both have work to do," I whispered, not really meaning it.

Sebastian chuckled and I peeked out from under my eyelashes. With a single, swift move he scooped me into his arms. A few steps and we were in our tiny bedroom at the foot of our too small bed.

With more gentleness than one would think from a man his size, he laid me on the bed and pressed his body onto mine, our hearts seeming to beat in time with one another.

"I love you, Sebastian," I whispered as he slid into me, completing me, making us one.

"I love you too, my bumpy, hive-ridden woman," he whispered into my ear, before biting it. I slapped him half-heartedly on the shoulder, and the sweet lovemaking quickly turned into a laughing romp that ended as it often did: in each other's arms, tears prickling at the back of my eyes as my emotions filled me and spilled over in physical release.

"You okay, Mara?" He touched a hand to my cheek, wiping away a tear.

"Yes," I curled deeper into his arms, trying to think of something smart to say and coming up empty handed so I settled for the truth. "Sometimes, I just love you so much, it makes me cry."

"Hmm. I am quite the hunk. Really, you are a rather lucky lady to have snagged me. I was planning on playing the field 'til I was at least sixty before you came along." He spread his big hands over his chest and leaned back against the headboard, a self-satisfied smile across his face. I smiled up at him, laughed, and shook my head. The size of his ego never ceased to amaze me.

Sobering, I sat up, and pulled the sheet around me.

"I'm going to ask the doctor about that Nevermore shot. I think it's what we've been waiting for. I mean, we could be fit, trim, and then have a baby, too. It would be amazing. Don't you think?" I stared at him, willing him to catch my excitement.

It didn't work. Sebastian frowned, and then shrugged his big shoulders. "I still think it's some sort of hoax, but ask him. See what he has to say, but don't get your hopes up. Please."

I wrapped my arms around him and snuggled into his arms. I could be excited enough for the both of us; in fact, I already was. My eyelids drooped as the double dose of antihistamines kicked in. I let my eyes close. For the first time in in a long time, my heart was light with the hopes and dreams of a family.

CHAPTER FOUR

Sebastian

Mara made an appointment the next morning and as luck would have it she got in on a cancelation for a couple of days later.

"You see? It's meant to be." She touched my cheek and I frowned.

"You are going to research Nevermore between now and then right? Maybe that person who cancelled had a valid reason for doing so."

She rolled her eyes but went straight to the computer. "Of course I am. I have faith though. This is the best thing for us."

True to her word, she spent the next two days researching the new drug before her appointment. What she found only solidified her reasoning. She pointed out paper after scientific paper hailing Nevermore as a miracle drug. "See? It's been tested and it's a good thing I got in on that cancellation. The back-up for the shot is huge. They're going into high production for it as we speak." She shook a paper at me and I smiled. I was nervous about new stuff like this. But I would support her. She was right, the medical community seemed to be all over the new drug.

The next day Mara left early for the doctor's office. The spring in her step was hard to see because ... well, because I had a bad feeling about this despite all the papers she'd found. If the Nevermore shot was a hoax, her heart would be broken. If it wasn't a prank, and yet still wasn't the fertility cure all she hoped, that would be even worse. I sighed and stared at the computer screen in front of me.

A blinking light came up in my inbox. "New client, or complaint from Gran that I don't call often enough?" I was betting on the latter. Gran was never happy with the amount of times I called. I could call her every day, and she would still complain I was a bad grandson. I grinned to myself and picked up the phone. The landline was scratchy, and I dialed through to my Gran.

She picked up on the second ring. "I don't need no damn life insurance so stop calling me, you dirty wankers."

"Well, Gran, don't you want to die and leave your favorite, handsome, and don't forget poor, grandson some money?"

"Oh, you cheeky buggar!" Her English accent came through more when she cussed at me and I couldn't help but laugh.

"You love me, don't deny it."

"Sass, you have too much sass for your own good. One day you'll get knocked down a peg or two. What's going to happen then?" She snorted softly. "And what are you doing, calling me in the middle of the day?"

"Mara had to go out, and I was betting that an email sent to me was probably from you. Cursing the likes of your only grandson who you love the best, but can't stand that he doesn't contact you more. You know, a gentle reminder as you like to do." I twisted the chord from the phone over one finger, staring blankly at the screen in front of me.

She snorted. "I didn't send you any email. So I hope you didn't bet a large amount of money on that."

"Ah, must be a new client then," I said as I clicked on the inbox. The email blinking back at me was not what I expected. The results of fertility testing had come in from our doctor back in Edmonton.

Gran was chattering on about her book club and how they were all too posh to read anything good like a smutty romance, even though that was what she liked the best. But I couldn't focus on two things at once. "Gran, can I call you back?"

"Why would you call me if you're just going to hang up on me now?"

I sighed. "Gran, I will call you back as soon as I can. But I . . .I have to deal with this."

"Cheeky buggar." She hung up on me.

I couldn't help but grin, but as I clicked on the fertility results email, the grin slipped.

"Shit." All the oxygen seemed to be sucked out of

my lungs. All along, the doctors had been saying fertility issues were common, and there were lots of ways to work around them. We could try in vitro fertilization, we could get a surrogate to carry a child to term for us if things were really bad, there was always adoption. But all of that was assuming Mara was the one that had the issue and that we could afford the cost of any of those things. All which ranged between fifteen and twenty thousand dollars. We'd always assumed that Mara was the one with the issues. .

I printed out the email and stared at it. Stared at it hard.

I was the fertility problem apparently. Low sperm count, damage to the sperm that couldn't be reversed. And there wasn't much to be had for it. Unless we decided to use a sperm donor.

The idea of raising another man's child, a child that was part Mara's but not part mine, shot through me like a slice to the belly. Or maybe in this case, the balls. I put my head on the desk and put my hands on the back of my neck.

Somehow I could make this right. I sat up and stared at the computer. I clicked open the search again and typed in "nevermore drug." A list of information came up immediately, most of the praise for it coming from scientists around the world. The drug had been developed in a lab right in Canada, and while the initial reasoning for it had been a cure for cancer, it had quickly proven that it could do so much more than that.

I skimmed the articles, taking it all in. The name of the scientist who'd spearheaded the program, and his beautiful red-headed wife who apparently was quite sick. The reasoning behind his push to get the drug into the public's hands wasn't hard to see.

I read softly, out loud. "The early batches of Nevermore were used on mice afflicted with a variety of illnesses. In all the cases, the mice were able to overcome and survive with no major side effect." Over and over again, the same word played out. Unprecedented. The drug was like nothing the world had ever seen before. It unlocked capabilities in the human body, allowing it not only to heal itself, but to become a more efficient machine.

Then there were the testimonials. The celebrities taking it, those who had Parkinson's, those who had cancer, those who had eating disorders.

I continued to read out loud to myself. "I've never felt better in all my years. . . the pain is finally gone . . . I can't believe I can live without fear of dying before my time." That last was a bit of a stretch in my mind, but then again that quote had come from that family who gained fame over a sex tape. I shook my head. I couldn't find a lot about the fertility help.

An hour later, I was on the tenth page of the search when I found the original article posted on a medical journal. I pulled the piece up and skimmed until I found what I was looking for.

I printed the piece out and then took the papers with me and headed out to the back porch. So immersed was I in my search, I'd forgotten to eat breakfast and my stomach growled as I passed the kitchen. I grabbed a banana off the counter and took it with me.

"The effect on fertility is immediate. Sperm counts go up and previously unviable sperm return to full health. The ability to reproduce in instances that don't involve a physical malformation are apparent in all test subjects." There was more about the improvement of the female reproductive system, as well, about the ability to carry to term, about a healthier pregnancy, along with a few other things but I skimmed those. Since Mara wasn't the issue, it wouldn't matter as much.

But if both Mara and I got the shot, then that would help and it certainly wouldn't hurt that we'd both taken it. Wouldn't it?

I ran a hand over my face. I didn't want to tell her . . .not right away. Maybe we could just wait and see if Mara having the shot would be enough to help us get pregnant. Help her get pregnant.

I nodded to myself. It was a good plan, for now, but I could make it better. So I thought.

Yes, a good plan for now. I smiled and went back into the house. I felt a little bad about telling Mara that the drug wouldn't work. But that would make the surprise when I told her I got the shot all that much better.

I knew the wait list for the shot would be weeks at best. If I booked myself in right away, and had to back out later they wouldn't care. Someone else would take my spot. But if I didn't book, I'd be way behind if we decided I needed it. Feeling like I had the process all under control I picked up the phone and dialed the doctor's office.

"I'd like to make an appointment, please."

CHAPTER FIVE

Mara

The doctor's office was bursting at the seams. And I don't mean all the seats were taken, I mean there wasn't even standing room in the tight spaces of the hallway.

I ended up halfway down the hall, leaning against the cream-colored wall next to one of the office doors. I had no doubt as to why there were so many people there. The treatment room looked like a revolving door with the people going in and out every few minutes.

"Excuse me, are you Mara Wilson?" a voice behind me asked.

I turned to face a woman who looked vaguely familiar. She was in her late thirties with beautiful blond hair and eyes the color of the Caribbean ocean. I cocked my head to one side, doing my best to place her. "Yes, I'm Mara. I'm sorry, have we met?"

The woman laughed and patted me on the arm. "Only briefly and it was a few months back. I'm Shelly Gartlet. I live on the road above you. We met at the mailbox when you first moved here, remember?"

I smiled and nodded. "That's right. I do remember now."

Really, how could I forget? The woman had grabbed me in a welcoming hug, spilling all the neighborhood gossip in less than five minutes, and in a single breath. Including several affairs that were going on, a man who'd lost his tree-cutting business, and as well as the scoop on Dan who'd she'd referred to as crazier than a bag of peanuts. I think she'd meant nuttier, but I didn't correct her at the time. Instead, I'd made a mental note never to confide in her.

"Are you here for the Nevermore shot?" I asked. "I mean, if that isn't too personal."

Shelly smiled. "Yes and no. My husband, George, and I got the shot last week, but Jessica here," she half tugged a younger looking clone forward, "wasn't able to get the shot, she was sick with that flu that's been going around."

I put my hand out to Jessica, surprised and wondering just why she would need the shot. Maybe she had cancer? That was one of the things the shot took care of. I hoped that was not the case, though I suppose if it was, the Nevermore shot would heal her as it had done so many others. Jessica was a beautiful young girl. She had the same long blonde hair as her mom and the same bright stunning eyes. She looked to be about sixteen years old, but could have been younger or older; it was so hard to tell with the way girls dressed now. No doubt the boys went crazy for her at school. "Nice to meet you, Jessica." She gripped my hand lightly and ducked her head shyly.

Shelly patted her on the arm and gave me a wink. "Jessica, weren't you telling me about Mara's husband, and about how good-looking he is?"

Jessica flushed from her tiny pointed chin to the roots of her hair. Her eyes widened with what I could only assume was teenage horror as our gazes connected.

"I didn't mean . . . it's not like . . . Mom, how could you say that?" she finally spit out before turning back to me. "Honestly, it's not. . .he was very nice to me when I met him the other day."

I laughed softly and shook my head. "Don't worry about it." A part of me was pleased by the thought. I knew my husband was an attractive man, and it was nice when other people thought so too. Even if it was a teenager who had a crush on him. Despite the extra weight he carried, he was a tall, dark, and handsome guy who moved through the world with confidence and a wicked sense of humor. I knew he had women swooning over him in every age bracket. "It's okay, Jessica. I'm sure Sebastian would love to know he had an admirer."

"Please don't tell him," she whispered, but I didn't get a chance to respond. We were interrupted by a woman who pushed her way into our conversation.

"You here for that miracle drug?"

She was a chubby woman in her mid to late forties.

She stood so close behind me that there was no way she could have missed a single word of our conversations. A quick glance and from my experience and time in Weight Watchers, I knew she had to be at least eighty pounds overweight.

"Yes, I am actually. Is that what you are here for?" I asked.

"Hell, no. I'm perfect just the way I am." With her hands on her hips, and her purple and red muumuu fluttering around her thick ankles, she glared at me, daring me to call her out. I smiled and bit my tongue. She continued her rant, "All you yahoos coming in for some quick-fix are going to get what's coming to you. There's no such thing; it's ridiculous to think one shot can do all that. Fertility, heart stuff, making bones stronger—foolishness you've all bought into and handed over hard earned money for."

Shelly and Jessica backed away from the woman, and I smiled at them as I also gave the riled-up muumuu woman some room. In fact, everyone around her started to back off.

"Come over for coffee, Shelly," I said over the muumuu woman's head, "and we can get to know each other. Anytime, I would love some company." Shelly and Jessica smiled and they gave me identical thumbs up. This was one of the nice things about where we lived. Yes, we were in the country, but there were still neighbors close enough if you needed some sugar or a helping hand, or maybe just a cup of coffee with the local gals, they were not too far away. I smiled to myself. There were parts of the island that I loved, like the sense of community. Much as I struggled with certain aspects—like the broom plant—I was starting to believe that the island was everything I'd hoped for when we'd settled on it. A home. A community. A family.

"Mara Wilson?" The desk nurse called me and I followed her directions into the doctor's room, happy to get away from the woman on her tirade. I glanced back and she hadn't paused for a second and was now laying into a pudgy teenager on the other side of the hall. The doctor's room was close enough that I could still hear her with the door not completely closed, her voice rising with intensity.

"Exercise and diet. When I was young, kids were outside playing and working. None of this TV and computer crap." There was a pause and I imagined a nurse speaking to her. "No, I will not lower my voice; I think you all have lost your damn minds. This is some government conspiracy to plug you all full of tracking devices and drugs so they can better control us."

I shook my head. Why couldn't she just let all those who wanted to make their lives better alone? It was obvious she was delusional. She could use the shot and lose a few pounds, and she'd probably live longer. There was a large thump that rattled the wall and made me jump. Then came a god-awful screech that sounded like a parrot being strangled followed by a dull cheer from the crowded hall.

"You can't kick me out!" the woman screamed. "I have an appointment! I need my medications!"

Ejection from a doctor's office? That was a first for me. She probably really did need her meds.

I laughed at the absurdity of her claims. Health Canada and the FDA wouldn't allow a drug to be given to the masses if it hadn't been tested. They knew it was safe and there was no way it could get to the public unless it was good to go.

Ridiculousness, that was all she had going for her.

"Hello, Mara." Dr. Cooper stepped into the office, his gray hair and stooped shoulders making me wonder how much longer I would be able to go to him. In a strange twist of fate, my doctor from Edmonton had moved to the island six months before Sebastian and I. Of course, when I knew we were moving, I'd made sure I could get on his client list. He'd been my doctor a long time, and he'd seen me through my first miscarriage.

I trusted him completely.

"Hi, Dr. Cooper." I smiled, unable to suppress my emotions. This was it; this was the moment I'd been waiting for.

"I suppose you're here for the Nevermore shot?" he asked, his face a mask of concentration.

I smiled wider, my excitement spilling over into my words. "Yes, I can't tell you how happy I am that this has come along. It's perfect really. I can lose the last of the weight you said I should, in order to be at an optimum size for getting pregnant, and the shot will make me more fertile, right? That's what I heard on the radio and when I looked it up on the Internet it confirmed that. And then maybe Sebastian should get it too? Because you weren't sure if the fertility issues were with him or me. We could both take it and then we'd be sure to get pregnant, right? Sorry, I know I'm rambling. I'm just so happy; I can't believe this is finally going to happen. I'm going to be able to have a baby." I took a deep breath, realizing that I'd spoken at a rate of speed that was unusual even for me.

Because a tiny piece of me feared he was going to tell me that the fertility claims were false. That the shot didn't work that way.

Dr. Cooper didn't answer right away; his eyes stared at the screen of his computer as he scrolled through it, page by page, looking at my charts.

"Dr. Cooper? This is a good thing, right?" I was starting to get a bad feeling that maybe Sebastian was right; maybe this was all a horrible trick to make people hand over their money. Thinking that the muu-muu woman could have been right made my belly tighten with anxiety. No, there were too many people in the waiting room, and too many were going into the treatment room for their shots. Shelly and Jessica were here too, and she'd said that she and her husband had gotten the shot only the week before. If it was all a hoax, she wouldn't have said that. And it'd be all over the Internet and news. Wouldn't it?

My mind spun over and over as I tried to calm my fears. Dr. Cooper's voice slowed me down.

"Mara, the drug does all that and more. It strengthens bones giving them better density, it prevents skin cancer, and does increase fertility. Parkinson's and arrhythmias are virtually wiped out. It truly is a miracle drug, of that I have no doubt. I am encouraging as many patients as possible to take it. The toll on the medical system from these issues alone is immense and they are about to disappear."

I let out a breath I didn't know I'd been holding in a huge sigh of relief, my heart slowing to a normal rhythm. I folded my hands over my heart and leaned forward. "You scared me. I thought you were going to tell me it was some sort of an Internet hoax. That's what Sebastian thought it was, some scam to get money out of people."

Dr. Cooper shook his head, but he still wasn't smiling, and that made me nervous again. "It's no hoax, Mara." He paused and I smiled. He didn't smile back. "But, you can't take the shot. I'm so sorry, my dear."

A loud buzz filled my ears, and though Dr. Cooper continued to talk, I couldn't hear a word he said. I blinked once, twice as I grasped the words, and fully processed them.

"Wait, why not?" I whispered.

He let out deep sigh and held his hands out to me. I gave them to him and he cupped them gently, like a kind grandfather would.

"Nevermore is derived from cystius scoparius. Do you know what that is?"

I stared at him, confusion rushing through me. "I don't. What is it? Is it bad?" *Sheesh, Mara, obviously it is bad since whatever it is means you can't take the drug.*

His eyes were sad and filled with compassion. "Cystius scoparius is more commonly known as Scotch Broom. The concentrate within the drug would kill you at worst, and at best, you would be in a constant state of agony, hives, sinus infections, swollen glands, and hypersensitivity to the mildest of irritations. There have even been some reported cases where people who were allergic to broom took Nevermore and now they've lost their eyesight." He squeezed my suddenly ice-cold hands. "You can't take Nevermore, Mara. In good conscience, I cannot allow you to proceed with this."

My mind whirled, hopes thrown about in a tornado of emotions before they crashed and burned. I pulled my hands slowly away from him and folded my arms across my breasts, at a loss for words, the weight of what he was saying pinning my heart to the floor.

Dr. Cooper leaned back in his chair and slid a sheet toward me. "Here's the chemical breakdown, Mara. Every aspect of the broom has been used in this drug, not just part of it."

"Why are you giving this to me?" I asked, trying to keep the venom that welled up within me out of my voice. The paper trembled in my hands.

He drew in a breath and slowly let it out before he answered. "Because I know you, Mara. I know how much you want children, and how hard you've worked to lose the weight that was preventing that dream. I know that after two miscarriages you feel like this is the end of your hope because of the financial situation you and Sebastian are in. You're going to try and find a way around this. You need to understand this clearly. I don't want you to die—and that is most likely what will happen if you take Nevermore because of how sensitive you are to the allergen. There is no way around this." His voice was so soft, and gentle, that it broke down the last barrier of strength I'd propped up, and a sob slipped past my clenched lips.

"I'm so sorry, Mara," he said, and I bit back the next cry that bubbled up my chest. I stood and ran to the door, pushing past the horde of people that filled the hallway, running half blind with tears until I reached my car. I leaned against it, head on the hot metal while my wild heart rate slowed. Dr. Cooper was right. This wasn't the end of the world; it really didn't make it any harder for Sebastian and me to have a baby. At least, that's what I told myself.

"Got the shot, did you?" a rather familiar voice threw the question at me.

I spun on my heel to face down the chubby muu-muu woman who'd been tossed out of the clinic. She was at the back door of my car, only a couple of feet from me. I pulled myself up tall.

"Not that it's any of your business, but no, I didn't," I snapped, forcing back the urge to push her away from me.

She nodded. "Smart girl. I'll tell you now, it was the best decision you ever made. The government won't get you now." She reached out and patted me on the arm. I shrugged her hand off and bit my tongue. The four letter words that wanted to spill out would have only left me screaming and ranting at the unsuspecting woman. And even though she was obviously unstable, and I was heart sick, I wouldn't let myself go that far.

I unlocked the car, slid into my seat, and started the engine. The rearview mirror gave me a perfect picture of the purple muumuu waddling through the parking lot toward the front doors of the clinic. The woman was probably on her way to accost another person leaving the clinic and tell them all the reasons they were wrong. That they had made a bad choice.

"It wasn't a choice I made. It was a choice taken from me," I whispered to her retreating figure. I took a deep breath and headed home to Sebastian and the farm.

CHAPTER SIX

Sebastian

One look at Mara as she stepped into the house said it all. But I still asked. "What happened?"

"Allergic to the . . .drug. It would kill me." She fell into my arms and I caught her, crushing her to my chest.

"Baby, it'll be okay." I closed my eyes and pressed my mouth to her head, breathing slowly. I couldn't tell her I was getting the shot. Not now. What if I had the same issue? Or what if it didn't work? I couldn't raise her hopes and then crush them again. I would get the shot, and then we'd see what happened. Thank God I'd made the appointment when I did.

The surprise and joy on her face when she finally was able to hold a baby would be worth all these tears. I rubbed her back. "It will be okay. I know it will."

She hiccupped a sob and pushed away from me as

she shook her head. "You don't understand. You aren't the one who had to get a D&C, you aren't the one who had doctors poking and prodding as they took away what was left of the baby."

I frowned at her. "I lost them too, Mara."

"It isn't the same," she whispered, tears tracking down her cheeks.

"You think I didn't grieve?"

Her lips tightened. "No. You never cried, you never said anything. You just moved on. Like you always do, like nothing bad happened. Like it didn't matter either way."

I put a hand to the door beside me, steadying myself. "That's not fair. They were mine too."

She shook her head and ran up the stairs to the bedroom. The door slammed, echoing through the house. The intellectual part of my brain told me she was lashing out because she was so upset. That she didn't really mean what she was saying. Yet, I knew people spoke truth when they were angry or hurt. Maybe they never would have said it out loud otherwise, but that didn't make it any less true.

No different than speaking to someone who'd had a few drinks, and the alcohol had firmed up their spines.

I headed to the kitchen, grabbed a couple of beers from the fridge and strode out of the house. I didn't really know where I was headed, and I just kept moving. The bright yellow broom bushes were starting to wilt, and I almost welcomed them brushing against me. A good reason not to rush home to Mara.

"Damn it, Mara."

I climbed the hill that led to Dan's place, and it wasn't long before his house came into view.

Holding the beers in one hand, I rapped my other hand on the one door that led into the house. "Hey, Dan, want a beer?"

There was no sound, no noise of someone running to greet me. I snorted to myself. Not like Dan would run to greet me like my drinking buddies back in Edmonton.

Though, where the old dude was ... that in itself was a mystery. "Thought you said you didn't leave the property often?" That's what he'd told me. Apparently, I had excellent timing.

I let out a sigh and looked around the yard. The afternoon made for some nice shade, and it wasn't like I had anywhere else to go. I twisted off the cap of one of the beers and took a long swallow. The bitter cold soothed my dry mouth and I let out another sigh.

I found a place near the garden in the shade and I lay back on the grass and stared up at the canopy above. I still couldn't believe Mara thought I wasn't upset by the miscarriages. I mean . . . did she think I was that cold? Or that I didn't give a shit?

I threw my arm over my eyes and took another long drag of beer.

Somewhere between the last drag of beer and

thinking about opening the next, I closed my eyes. I just wanted to block the world out for a minute.

"Hello?"

The soft-pitched word shot me straight up. Blinking, I looked across the yard at the young girl standing at Dan's door.

"He's not here."

She gasped and spun around. I'd met her before at the local grocery store. Her mother had been very excited to meet me and had even hugged me after speaking to me for all of two minutes. The long blonde hair and blue eyes just like her mom's were a dead giveaway. Crap, what was her name?

I took a stab at it. My memory was awful. "Janice?"

She gave me a shy smile. "Jessica. Do you know where Dan is? My mom asked me to come over and see if he wanted to have dinner with us."

I raised my eyebrows. "Really?"

She shrugged. "My parents are very religious and they believe in making everyone feel welcome."

"Hmm." I nodded, though I wasn't sure I'd invite Dan for dinner. Helpful as he'd been with the gardening stuff, he wasn't much of a conversationalist. "Well, you can wait with me for him if you want."

Jessica slowly approached me like she wasn't sure she should stick around. "Okay."

"Or I can give him the message. Totally up to you." I cracked the top on the second beer. Dan was out of luck.

The kid sat across from me. "I saw your wife at the clinic today."

I grimaced. "Yeah, that didn't go too well."

She blinked those big blue eyes up at me and scooted a little closer. "Why not?"

I looked over her shoulder to Dan's house, letting my mind replay the scene from a mere hour before. "She couldn't get the shot."

"Oh. That's too bad."

I shot a look to her. The tone of her words was ... off. "Yeah, it is."

"Can I have a drink?"

"Thought your family was religious? I don't want to get you in trouble."

She smiled. "I drink when I want with my friends."

Her hand shot out and she snatched the beer from me before I could stop her. Damn her reflexes were fast. She tipped the beer back and swallowed several gulps.

I leaned back on my elbows, doing my best not to think about if she were my kid. I moved the conversation back to its original course. "How often do you have Dan over for dinner?"

She took another swig of beer before she answered. "Once a month. You and your wife will probably be put on the schedule too."

I laughed. "The schedule?"

She nodded. "My mom likes to make sure all the neighbors feel they are important. It's stupid if you ask me. Dan only shows up for the free food. He doesn't even talk. Unless my dad says something about the military or politics and then they just argue."

"Sounds like fun." I held my hand out for the beer

and she laughed and took another big gulp, leaving only maybe one sip left at the bottom. I motioned for her to finish it up. I didn't need any kid's backwash. Well, maybe my own one day if Mara and I could ever actually get pregnant.

I wondered if she'd come out of the bedroom yet. Or if she'd even noticed I'd left the house.

"Hey, I asked you what you do for fun?"

I barely glanced at the girl. "I work a lot. I don't have time for fun stuff."

"Well, that's no good. We could have fun together."

I shrugged, not really hearing her words. I mean I heard them, but I didn't get what she was getting at. "Yeah, whatever."

There was movement in the bush at the side of the house. Dan stepped out and his eyes shot to us. I lifted a hand. "Seriously, I thought you never left your house?"

Dan grunted, and then his eyes shot to Jessica. "What do you want, girl?"

Her lips turned down, and she just twisted so she could shout at him. "My mom wants you to come to dinner tonight. I think you should decline."

The old guy grunted. "Tell her I'll be there at six."

Jessica shot to her feet and stomped off. She threw a glance back at me and mouthed something that could have been 'later,' but I was already up and moving toward Dan.

He slid his gun and a pack off his back.

Curiosity got the better of me. "Were you hunting?"

"Manner of speaking."

"What does that mean?"

"Means I was checking on things. Something weird is going on." He glanced at me. "And watch out for that kid, she's trouble."

I twisted around to where Jessica had disappeared. "Her?"

"Yeah. Her. She's got a thing for the older men."

I burst out laughing at the joke. "Fuck off."

He gave a half laugh. "You think I'm joking. Kid came onto me at one of her family dinners. Had her hand halfway up my thigh before I realized what was happening."

I stared at him, doing my best to see through the grizzled exterior. Okay. Sure. If he cleaned up--he probably was only in his later forties and obviously in good shape. But Jessica couldn't have been more than fourteen or fifteen. "No fucking way. Are you sure you aren't making that shit up? Maybe having a lucid dream?"

One beer on an empty stomach was getting to me. I never swore. Never. And here I was dropping f-bombs like they were part of my usual lingo. Or maybe I was just still pissed about what Mara had said.

If I was honest, that was the real root of my anger.

"Just watch yourself. That is, if you like your marriage the way it is, and your ass out of jail."

I drew myself up. "I'm not interested in anyone but my wife. And certainly not some kid barely out of diapers."

He gave me a sharp nod. "Good. Now, what are you doing here?"

I shook my head. "Just . . . wanting to learn more about living rural. You seem to be the guy to talk to."

Dan chewed the stub of his cigar for a moment. "Good idea. Way things are going, the world is going to end before we know it."

I laughed. He didn't. With a quick jerk, he pulled his backpack onto his back. "You got a food storage? Weapons? Is your house fortified?"

I stood staring at him for a moment as his words processed. "Ah, no not all of that. We fixed the fencing around the acreage. It's that nice square page wire." I held my hands about six inches apart. "Squares spaced like this to keep the animals out."

"You're going to need more than that." He tipped his head and opened the door to his house. I followed him in. The basement was cool like a cold storage.

"I've got enough rations here to last a few years. Enough ammo to stay holed up for as long as the food lasts. Water pipes above collect rain from the roof and run through a purification system."

I looked around at the carefully labeled shelving units. The food was stocked in row upon row, dated and set in alphabetical order from what I could see.

I found myself drawn into his conspiracy theory world. "How do you run the purification system?"

"Solar powered panels on the roof."

And so the afternoon was spent with me going through the house with him, discussing ways to make Mara and my property more "water tight" as Dan put it. He gave me a couple of books that talked about the breakdown of society when things went wrong. What would be lost first. How the infrastructure, government, and army would collapse. I hated to admit that the whole thing intrigued me.

Books in my arms, I headed home as the sun set. The bush I pushed through was suddenly not so friendly looking as the length of the shadows grew and the sounds of the local wildlife clattered around me. As long as it wasn't Bob the bear, I would be fine. With that thought, I hurried my feet.

Home though was far from welcoming. The lights were all out. There was no movement. My shoulder's slumped as I thought about what I faced.

I let myself into the house and flicked on the kitchen light. Putting the books on the table, I steeled myself. Maybe I didn't grieve the way Mara did, but that didn't mean I hadn't been hurt too.

I smiled to myself. It would be okay. I'd told her that and ultimately I believed it. I'd get the Nevermore shot. We'd have as many babies as she wanted.

Life would be amazing.

Chapter Seven

Mara

The darkness of the room held me close, and I let it cover me, let it hide me from the grief of losing my dreams of being a mother. Someone said that depression over something as minor as this was silly, that I should just shake it off and get out of bed. I closed my ears, closed my mouth, and drifted back to sleep.

CHAPTER EIGHT

Sebastian

The first couple of weeks that Mara hid in the room, I let her. Partly because I was keeping myself busy with work. Partly because I was keeping an eye out for all the things Dan had tipped me off to.

Conspiracy theories abounded on the Internet and I found myself sucked into them for hours at a time after I was done with my client websites. I'd print out the latest thing and then walk over to Dan's place. We'd discuss the viability of the theory, share a beer, and then I'd go home and try to get Mara out of bed.

Most times I ended up just lying beside her, holding her close while she dozed in my arms. I wasn't sure what I was going to do. I couldn't get her to even phone the counselor she saw after the first miscarriage.

She was wallowing in the pain. She gave me all sorts of excuses that had nothing to do with the letdown of not getting the shot, but they were just that—excuses.

I needed to do something drastic.

A month into her self-imposed confinement, I had a day planned that would change everything.

More than I realized at the time.

First, I had my scheduled doctor appointment. With more than a little trepidation, I headed into Nanaimo, the only place I could get in for the shot. The receptionist asked me to sit in the waiting room along with a dozen or more other people. There was a low buzz of talking in the backdrop from the receptionist. She had her head bent low over the phone.

I picked up a word or two, none of them good.

"No . . .shots."

"Nevermore . . .pulled."

"I'll tell them."

The receptionist stepped out from behind her glass divider. Her name tag said Joy, but she looked nothing like her namesake at the moment. Heavyset, her uniform pulled over her body in awkward angles made worse every time she tugged at it.

"I'm sorry," she said softly, "the clinic will not be giving out any Nevermore shots today. We're out of stock."

Those around me gasped and after quite a bit of arguing with Joy, who did her best to soothe them, explaining they would be notified when another batch of the drug came in. But I didn't think that was happening. I'd overheard enough of the conversation Joy had on the phone and I knew there wouldn't be a tomorrow.

Finally, after much persuasion, the rest of the patients left. I just sat there, disbelief coursing through me.

No, I wouldn't take no for an answer. I couldn't, and for Mara, I would do everything I could to make this happen, no matter the reason the drug was pulled. How bad could it be? Over half the world has taken it.

I approached the desk and peeked around the divider at Joy. She stared at her paperwork, doing her best to ignore me. Not easy as I was leaning in as far as I could.

"Joy, is there not even one vial left in the clinic?"

She shook her head and glanced up at me. "I'm sorry."

"My wife . . . we just want to have a family. This is probably our only chance. I've already paid for the shot." Silently I was begging her to look up.

Her shoulders slumped inside her pink uniform. "I'm so sorry. I was supposed to get Nevermore today, too. You can get a refund at the front desk from the receptionist there."

Now my shoulders slumped. "Joy, please. I can't . . .I can't leave without getting that shot. Please help me. Help me and my wife. Please."

Her light green eyes flicked to mine and she drew a breath. I put all I could into keeping her eyes locked on mine, on showing her that I was serious. I laid out all my cards.

"Joy, we've had two miscarriages, and on top of that I . . .my swimmers are drowning if you know what I mean. My wife is so depressed, I can't get her out of bed, please . . . please, help me."

She closed her eyes. "I could lose my job. They pulled the drug."

"Why?"

She shook her head. "No reason that they are giving. Probably a price jack." She slapped a hand over her mouth. "Please, don't tell anyone I said that."

"I can't afford more than what they're charging," I whispered. "Please, is there anything you can do? Anything at all?"

Joy stood and came around to look into the waiting room, which was now completely empty. "Maybe. Just . . .wait here."

She turned and walked down the hall, through a swinging door at the end that went to one of the treatment rooms. I drummed my fingers on the wall, hoping.

Then again, maybe she was going to get the security guard I'd seen out front of the clinic. I frowned. No, I had to believe . . .

Joy came back with a small bag in her hands. "It's on ice. I can't give it to you, but you can do it yourself. In the thigh would be best."

I peeked into the bag. A small vial and a single needle stared up at me. "Why?"

She shrugged. "Because I . . .understand depression and losing babies. I wish my husband had been as driven as you to help me. Maybe we would have stayed together."

I swallowed hard, my throat burning more than a little. "And I can give it to myself?"

"It's that or not at all. Right in the thickest part of the muscle," she whispered.

Impulsively, I hugged her. "Thank you. And he was a fool to leave you when you needed him most."

"I know, and good luck," she whispered. "I've got a package like that for myself. Go. They are counting the last of the batch now."

I gave her a smile, backed up, and hurried out of the clinic as fast as I could go without running.

In my beat up old car, I stared at the bag. With trembling fingers, I pulled out the container and stared at it. Carefully, I drew the contents of the vial into the needle, then tapped the side of the syringe, which sent bubbles to the top. I mean, I'd seen a hundred movies, TV shows, and the like where shots were given. I paused and pulled up a tutorial on the Internet to make sure I was doing it right.

Then again maybe I was just stalling. It was one thing to have another person give you a shot, totally different to do it yourself.

I rubbed my hand over my face and pulled up the edge of my shorts to reveal the pasty white thigh underneath. "Do it man. Just do it!" I barked the words, thinking of Dan for some strange reason.

I pressed the needle against the skin, felt the pop of flesh giving way to the sharp point. I sucked in a breath at the quick pain, and then depressed the plunger.

Nevermore serum shot out all around the head of the needle. "What the hell?" I pulled the needle out and stared at it. Did another quick Internet search and then twisted the needle to tighten the head.

"I'm an idiot." I muttered. There was only about three-quarters of the syringe full now. I could only hope it would be enough. I went through the same process again and finally got the serum into me.

A hot flush of tingles shot through my leg within seconds of pulling out the needle. I pressed my finger over the tiny puncture wound and leaned my head back against the seat. The tingles flowed in every direction, and I couldn't believe the energy that came with them.

And the instant need for a cheeseburger. I drew a breath. I could grab something on the way to my next stop.

Chewing on my third burger, I headed to the closest pet store.

Maybe we couldn't have a human baby right away, but that didn't mean I couldn't take home something to love that was like a baby.

I stepped into the pet store, the smell of small animals and the racket of birds assaulting my ears. This was no time to be coy. I went straight to the cashier. He was a young kid, tall and gangly with a spattering of acne on his forehead.

I put my hands on the counter. "I need a puppy for my wife."

"Got in trouble, did you?" The kid winked at me and I rolled my eyes.

"Do you have any puppies, right now?"

"Nope. But I have a friend out in Errington that just had a litter of yellow labs about eight weeks ago. Want me to see if they have any left?"

Thank God. "Yes."

A quick phone call later and I had an address and the cash for the puppy. Mara's family had grown up with Dobermans, but I knew she liked all dogs. Especially puppies.

The farm where said puppies were was a half hour north of Nanaimo, deep in the rural section of Errington. I missed the driveway twice before I realized it was even a driveway.

Potholed and full of bumps, the path shook my little car so hard, I was sure I heard screws shake loose. "Better be the cutest damn puppy in the world," I muttered.

An older couple waved at me as I pulled in. They looked a bit like Ma and Pa Kettle, right down to the overalls on him and the long printed flower dress on her. I snorted to myself and stepped out of the car.

"Hello—"

"This way." The older man cut me off and headed toward the big old barn behind the house.

Not exactly friendly but what did I know. As we passed the house, the wall closest to me shuddered, like something large slammed into it. I jumped and stood staring. The window to the left was boarded up with no glass in the frame.

A hand reached between the slats.

"I said, this way." The old guy grabbed my arm and dragged me past the window as a second hand emerged and reached for me. A yellowed hand, as if the person connected had jaundice.

"What—"

"You want the puppy or not? Giving them away now."

I stumbled after him, more than stunned into silence. Errington was known for hosting some weirdness. But this was above and beyond.

The barn door was open and the musty air spilled out toward me. There was a woof from the depths.

"It's okay, Missy." The old guy's voice softened as he hurried across the barn. "This is the last pup, all the rest are gone." He scooped up a puppy and all but pushed him into my arms. "Take him."

I clutched the puppy to my chest and he wiggled in my arms. The mother, Missy, gave another woof and pressed herself against my legs. She had two big wounds on her back, almost like large bite marks. But that couldn't be right because . . . they looked like a person had bitten her.

"What about the mom?" I wanted to take her, too, as it was more than obvious that she was being neglected.

The guy's shoulders tightened. "You want Missy?"

She woofed and I nodded, pulling myself up to my full height so I could look down on him. Normally I wouldn't use my height to intimidate. But this time . . .

"Yeah, I do. My wife loves dogs. She hates to see them suffer." I dropped a hand to Missy's head and she leaned into me.

"Fine, take them both. Just go."

I snapped my fingers at Missy and she heeled to my side like she'd been my dog for years. As we stepped into the sunlight, I couldn't help the feeling of being watched.

As we drew next to the house, Missy let out a low, rumbling growl, and every hair along her spine stood. I put a hand on her head then felt the hair on the back of my neck stand at attention.

I slowed next to the window, wanting another look. Because there was no way I wasn't reporting this to the police. But I needed more than a "things just seemed off and I think someone was locked in the house. And the dog has bite marks on it."

The wooden slats of the window were slammed and a roar from within the house sent me flying backward. Wood board creaked under the weight of a body and I caught a glimpse of a snarling face.

Images flickered through my mind.

Puppies running under my feet. Scooping them up. Eating them as they screamed.

The snarls of Missy as she fought for her pups.

I sucked in a sharp breath, gasping to get enough air. I felt like I was drowning. I ran for the car, Missy right behind me. I opened the driver's side door and she leapt in.

With the puppy clutched to my chest and Missy riding shotgun, I sped out of the driveway as fast as I could. Legs shaking, I didn't slow until I was on the main road. I pulled over and dialed 9-1-1.

The operator didn't answer.

"What the fuck?" I whispered. How could 9-1-1 not pick up?

Missy shoved her wet nose into my face and I rubbed her ears. "Nothing's going to happen to you two."

She gave a soft woof and the puppy in my arms squirmed. I looked down at him, seeing the scratches along his back. Like those from a set of fingernails grabbing at him and just missing.

"Holy shit, what did I just get you two out of?"

Two pairs of liquid brown eyes stared up at me. I put the puppy next to his mom and headed home.

I tried to get through to the police twice more with no luck.

All the way home, I did the best I could to calm myself. I couldn't tell Mara about this, not today. Maybe in a few months.

Or maybe never. It was too horrible to consider.

Worse . . . how had I seen those horrible images in my head?

CHAPTER NINE

Mara

On the twenty-eighth day of my—self-imposed—confinement, a booming rattle shook me awake, the bedroom door flinging open. I know the days exactly thanks to Bastian.

"That's it, twenty-eight days is long enough, Babe. I've been patient and done what I could, but you've got to get up," Sebastian barked as he whipped the covers off me.

"Leave me alone," I grumbled, grabbing at the blankets. He snatched them out of my hands.

"Nope, time to grow up and get with the program, beautiful lady. Today is a good day to be alive."

Bright sunlight streamed into the room as he opened all the curtains. "There's no use crying over something you can't change." He sat on the bed and pulled me upright to sit beside him.

"It isn't fair," I said, hating how childish I sounded. "Every crack head and addict out there can get pregnant, and they can't even take care of themselves. We would be able to give a child a life, a family, and a home."

Sebastian nodded. "I know, babe, but you're not doing yourself any good by wallowing in this."

I frowned at him. "I'm not wallowing."

"Yes, you are. I have something for you. Two somethings to be exact. But it's down in the garden so you'll have to haul your butt down there. I've got to go back into town. I'll be back in a couple hours."

I stood and stomped my way to the bathroom, brushing past him. "What do you know anyway? You're just a man. You don't have an internal clock like I do," I snapped as I turned on the shower and got in the steaming water. I knew I was being unfair. I wasn't stupid . . .I just . . . I didn't know how to not let this latest reality hurt me as badly as it was.

So I let my thoughts float to how ridiculous he was for thinking he knew better than me.

Stupid male, what did he know about really wanting babies? Or losing weight for that matter? The man thought he was a Greek god, the way he strutted through the house naked, preening in front of mirrors. I snorted to myself. My anger faded as I worked the soap through my hair, the hot water rinsing away the last of the tears. Gratitude flowed through me. Without his intervention and care, I'd still be in that bed. I had to admit, I was curious about just what could be in the garden waiting for me.

I smiled to myself. I'd have to be careful about how I thanked him, or I'd never hear the end of it.

Fifteen minutes later, I headed out the back door to the garden when a soft woof met my ears. I blinked, stared, and couldn't believe what I was seeing. Sitting next to the freshly dug earth, with a giant red ribbon tied around its neck, was a tiny yellow Labrador Retriever. And next to the tiny version was a larger version, obviously the momma by the way her teats hung low.

I clapped my hands over my mouth and the two dogs woofed at me together. The female leapt toward me first, licking at my hands. My eyes though went to the big open sores on her back. I went to my knees.

"Oh, you poor beauty." I hugged her around the neck, careful not to squeeze too hard.

The puppy ran up and crawled into my lap as he wriggled, his entire body wagging as if his tail alone wasn't enough. I scooped him up and held him close as he licked my face, his still-sweet puppy breath tickling me.

"Oh, you devil of a man," I said as I cuddled the two bundles of fur close to me. "What are we going to call you, hmm?" I rubbed the puppy's velvety soft ears and he settled down, resting his nose on the crook of my neck. I pressed my cheek against him. "How about Nero?" I'd grown up with a big yellow Lab my grandparents had rescued and named Nero. He'd been my companion and best friend for years.

The female lab wore an old leather collar. I tugged

it around until I could read the faded silver bit attached to it.

"Missy" was stamped into a homemade tag. "Missy?"

She woofed, her beautiful brown eyes blinking up at me. I had no doubt Sebastian hadn't been planning on two dogs . . . but the sores on Missy . . . there was no way he would have left her behind. He was as much a sucker for a rescue case as I was.

A voice called from the front of the house, "Hello? Mrs. Wilson?"

Missy let out a soft growl and put herself between me and the house.

I stood with Nero still in my arms. "Come on, let's see who it is."

Missy heeled at my side, tight like a burr to my pants. We walked around the house to see Jessica carrying a basket filled to the brim. She smiled at me over the basket, her eyes lighting on Nero and Missy.

"You've got a puppy? Oh, he's so cute. Can I hold him?" I handed him to her as she handed me the basket of goodies.

"It's a belated welcome-to-our-neighborhood gift," Jessica said as she snuggled with the wriggling puppy. Missy watched closely, but her growling had eased off.

"Thank you, that's really sweet," I said, placing the basket on the porch railing. Now that I was up and out of the house, the fresh air was giving me long waited for energy. That and my two new family members.

"Do you want to go for a walk with me, us?"

Jessica nodded and put him down. Missy sniffed

him over, and apparently satisfied, moved to walk in front of us with Nero at her back feet.

"Let me just grab a leash of some sort." I ran into the house and scrounged around until I settled on one of Sebastian's work ties. It would work in a pinch. Leash in hand, we walked on out the front drive, past the old iron gates that had hung for as long as the property had existed. They were heavy and sturdily built when the farm was started a hundred years before. Each panel was taller than I was and easily weighed a hundred pounds. The supports were cemented into the ground on either side, and there was a huge rusting metal bar that slipped into place to lock it. Scrolling leaves and grape clusters were welded on in an attempt to soften the hard steel lines, to make it look more artistic than prison-ish. The attempt didn't work well.

At the best of times, it was a major effort to close the thing, which is why we left it open, and why the bar was nearly covered in vegetation. Also why we planned to rip it out as we continued our renovation process.

Jessica chatted the entire time. Her bubbly personality yet another stamp of her mother's genetics coming through.

"So there's this guy I like," she said. "He's super nice and cute, and I think he likes me too."

I smiled at her. "Yeah? Does this guy have a name?"

She blushed and looked away. "I don't want to jinx myself. He's . . .he's got a girlfriend, you know. And she's . . . well, she's not very pretty."

My smile slipped a little. "Pretty isn't everything, Jessica. If she's a nice girl, that should be enough."

"Well, I guess. I just think he could do better. And nice . . . nice doesn't get you anywhere."

I had to blink my shock away quickly. She was a teenager, after all, but her words had the hard edge of a woman who'd been through a lot. "Maybe. But I don't really think you believe that, do you?"

She shrugged. "I think that if you want something, you should go after it, don't you?"

That I agreed with. "Of course, I do. But not at the expense of someone else."

We were at the far end of our road when a scream shattered the air. We both jumped and I scooped up Nero. Missy didn't bark, but cocked her head with her ears pricked toward the house to the right of us.

I swallowed hard. "Is that normal for them?"

Jessica drew a slow breath and shook her head. "I . . . I think they fight sometimes. My mom said they are on the verge of divorce."

There was a second explosion of sound, only this time it was a gun. I put a hand on Jessica's shoulder. "We have to call the police."

She nodded and we ran back the way we'd come. We had to pass Jessica's house. "Go, get inside and don't answer the door. I'll call the police."

Her eyes were wide and she didn't argue.

I ran back to our farmhouse, Missy at my side. Nero wasn't that big but I was out of shape from hiding in the bedroom. He seemed heavier than he really was by the time we got to the driveway.

I hurried up the back steps and let Missy in, put Nero down and went straight to the phone.

I dialed 9-1-1. An operator picked up on the second ring.

"I think one of my neighbors just shot . . ." Okay, I was going to assume here, "Just shot his wife."

I rattled off the address before I realized there was no one on the line. "Hello?"

An automated voice said, "Please be advised all emergency lines are currently down."

I stared at the phone and slowly put it back into the cradle. What did that mean?

Then I realized I wasn't alone in the house.

"Mara?"

"Bastian, I think one of our—"

"Yeah, I heard you. Honey. Come here."

I picked Nero up and hurried into the living room. Missy bounded ahead of me, shoving her nose into Sebastian's hand. He rubbed the top of her head absently. He sat glued to the TV.

I tapped him on the shoulder. "I can't believe you bought me a puppy but what happened to Missy—"

"Shhh," he cut me off and pointed to the TV.

On the screen was a reporter standing in front of Vancouver General Hospital. The voice that came over the TV was a bit high-pitched as though the reporter had either been kicked in the balls, or was extremely anxious. My bets were on the latter.

"It appears that the miracle drug, Nevermore, wasn't such a miracle after all. Early reports are just now coming in that in the most recent batches, due to an effort to keep up with demand, the toxins thought to be strained out of the main component of the drug—cystius scoparius, better known as Scotch Broom—were not eliminated. If you have received a shot in the last ten weeks, please report to your local authorities immediately."

A second reporter came on screen. She choked up even as her eyes misted over, and I wondered if she had taken the drug or knew someone close to her who had. "The toxins attack the part of the brain that makes a person human, whole sections of the cerebral cortex are eaten away until there is nothing left but a base animal instinct."

The image shifted to focus on someone—a patient, if the white cover up was any indication—stumbled out of the hospital. The reporter turned and ran toward the man who clutched at his stomach. She was pretty, and I wondered if she was nice too. I shook my head, that was just the conversation with Jessica rumbling around.

She pressed the microphone at him. "Sir, can you tell us why you're here today? Does it have anything to do with the Nevermore shot?"

"I'm so hungry, I can't stop eating. Nothing fills me up," he said. His eyes were glazed and his skin had a strong golden yellow hue to it, as if he had jaundice.

"Sir, did you take the drug Nevermore?" she asked, sticking the microphone even closer to the man.

He stared at the microphone for a moment, opened his mouth to answer, and then chomped his teeth around the fuzzy piece, growling and snarling.

Amplified by the microphone, the sounds roared through the TV. Missy snarled and dropped to her belly. With bared teeth, she lunged at the flat screen, smashing her nose into it.

"Missy, stop!" Sebastian grabbed her and tugged her back, but it was like she'd lost her mind. She continued to fight to get at the TV as the man's snarls echoed through the room. Nero cowered in my arms, whimpering.

Chills rippled over my body as Bastian wrestled with Missy. I put a hand on her head and she calmed right away. Trembling, she placed herself between me and the TV.

Sebastian kept a hand on her and we stared once more at the screen.

The reporter backed away from the snarling man and someone had turned off the microphone. The cameraman kept tabs on the man attempting to devour the equipment. Then the guy looked up, right into the camera as they zoomed in on him. His pupils twitched as the camera focused, sliding as we watched, from a perfect human round, to a horizontal rectangle, reminiscent of a goat's eye.

I gasped and grabbed for Sebastian's hand. He gave it to me and I clung to him. That could have been me if I'd taken the shot—would have been me if not for the main ingredient. I pressed my nose into Nero's fur and breathed in his scent as Sebastian's hand went clammy in mine. With my other hand, I kept stroking Missy's head. "Oh my God. Oh my God." I wasn't sure if it was a plea or a prayer that came out of my lips. Maybe one and the same.

The man with the now strange eyes and jaundiced skin stood and opened his mouth. I couldn't tell if he was trying to speak or if he roared at the camera. By the cameraman's reaction—jerking back and to the side—he was roaring. The scene jigged and jogged as the cameraman and the reporter fled, but in her heels and tight business skirt, the reporter wasn't fast enough. The camera turned in time to see her tackled from behind, her body slammed into the ground under the weight of the man who'd taken the Nevermore shot.

The man reared up and then came down hard with his mouth, ramming it into her back, ripping a chunk of flesh as if she were a loaf of bread. My eyes shot to Missy. The wounds in her back.

Sebastian's hand tightened on mine and my eyes shot back to the TV. The reporter's screams were audible from whatever mic was on the camera, then the camera was dropped and the screen scrambled, and then went black.

"That wasn't real," I said, though I knew already in my gut what we'd just witnessed had truly happened. It was like watching a hurricane rip apart a home on the news. You didn't think it was possible, didn't think they would air it, but in your heart you knew it wasn't staged.

Sebastian didn't say anything, he just flipped the channel. Every single one was breaking news and bulletins. The Nevermore drug had been taken by what officials estimated at close to ninety percent of the North American population over the last two months—street versions and FDA approved versions—both of which had the same effect because of the rate of production and the slip-shod method of getting it done. The only people not having issues were those who had taken the shot prior to the two-month mark. Which turned out to be only a few thousand people in the test market.

"We repeat, stay in your homes. Keep your doors locked. These are humans who have lost their humanity. We are working hard to find an antidote to this solution, to this issue. Please, do not attempt to stop those who've turned. They are not zombies, they are living, breathing creatures."

Sebastian snorted. "Issue? That's what this has been downgraded to?"

We watched in stunned silence for over an hour with the reports coming hard and fast at first, but then slowing. People were cautioned to stay within their homes and avoid all contact with the outside world. A clip of the reporter being attacked aired several more times, cutting out before the bite in her back actually happened.

"Sebastian, is that what happened to Missy?"

At the sound of her name, she lifted her head and yawned. The bites in her back flexed open as she stretched and other than a wince, she didn't seem to notice them.

"I think so. It's why I brought her home." He scratched her under the chin. "This is bad, Mara.

Really bad. It's like all of Dan's theories just came crashing down around us."

I hated to agree. "I never thought I'd see the day a zombie apocalypse would happen, though," I said softly as Sebastian turned the TV off.

"They aren't zombies," he snapped at me as he rubbed his left arm. "They can't bite you and turn you into one of them. The doctors on TV said that already."

"I didn't say they could turn us into them, I just . . . I don't know what to call them. Not-zombies? Nevermore monsters?" I was trying to lighten the mood, confused by his sudden turn of mood.

"No, you're right. I'm sorry; this has just really freaked me out," he said and pulled me into his arms. Nero squirmed in between us, and Missy added in her nose, too. I laughed softly at their insistence of being part of everything, and hugged all three.

"It'll be okay," I said. "We've got each other and the farm. We should be good for a while, right? It won't take long. Someone will have this straightened out in no time. I mean . . . maybe it will wear off? It's a shot, shots wear off."

Sebastian untangled himself from me and strode to the kitchen. "We have to be ready though. Dan is right about that."

I followed him, "For what?"

"I think we're going to be on our own for a while,"

he said as a loud thumping footstep echoed through our little house.

Missy let out a loud bark, followed by a low growl. She stared at the front door and pinned her ears back.

My adrenaline soared as I thought about the scene on the TV. The reporter hadn't had a chance, the speed of the Nevermore man and the ferocity of his attack were like nothing I'd seen before. No, that's not true. I'd seen a documentary about wolf packs. The way the wolves had shot out of nowhere to take down their prey . . . it was reminiscent of the speed of the once human man.

I swallowed hard and put Nero in the bathroom on a makeshift towel-bed, shut the door, and headed into the kitchen. I didn't want to believe we were already going to face down one of the Nevermores, but it was all too possible.

From the knife drawer, I pulled out the biggest blade and gripped it tightly. Sebastian nodded and pulled out a knife of his own. Together with Missy between us, we crept through the house to the front door, reaching it as another thump rumbled through the floorboards. What the hell was out there? I didn't want to know, really, I didn't.

Missy sniffed the air and shook her head. Almost like trying to tell us something, maybe not to open the door.

Sebastian held up his hand and with his fingers counted to three. I nodded. He held up one finger, two, and as he held up the third, he gripped the door-knob and snapped the door open.

CHAPTER TEN

Mara

D an stared at us with his eyebrows high. He had his gun slung over his shoulder and a strap across his chest full of long gold and silver cartridges. He looked like he had enough ammunition to take out half an army. And the cartridges looked big enough to drop an elephant. At least to my untrained eye.

Sebastian reached out and dropped a hand on Dan's shoulder. "Thank God, it was you and not one of those . . ."

Dan snorted. "You didn't know that though, did you?"

I pointed at Missy. "She did."

Missy sat between the three of us, happy as could be. Dan gave her a look. "Good idea to get a dog. Thing is, it ain't going to be enough. Not to survive what is coming. You got all those books still I gave you?"

He pinned Bastian with a look. All I could think was, what books? What had my husband been doing while I'd been cooped up in bed?

Dan put a hand on the doorframe. "Even with everything I've taught you, you still made a fatal error. You two need a lesson in surviving. First off, don't go investigating a strange noise without some serious firepower. This is not a horror movie. There's no hero coming to rescue you. You want to survive this outbreak of idiots who took some new drug and turned into animals, you're gonna have to do it on your own."

He stepped across the threshold and sauntered into our house, casual like, as if he belonged here. I lifted an eyebrow at Sebastian who shrugged. "Dan, what're you doing here?"

"Don't you listen, boy? You need a lesson or two before I go and lock myself in the bunker. I don't plan on coming out until after the winter and hope by spring some of this idiocy has passed." He paced the living room, peering out the curtains of the bay window.

I gripped the handle of my knife because his words stirred up an irrational fear that he was right. Dan couldn't be right. Dan was the crazy neighbor.

"Dan," I said, "they'll have an antidote in no time and this will go down as one of the greatest blunders in history and everything will go back to normal." I desperately wanted to believe my own words.

"You don't really believe that, do you, girl?" He

turned his steely eyes on me and I froze, my mouth dry as he made me face the reality with a single look.

I shook my head ever so slowly. He mimicked me, a wry twist on his lips. "Didn't think so." Flopping himself onto our couch, he motioned for us to come closer. Sebastian obeyed but I stayed where I was, next to the open door.

"Second thing, and you know this, boy," Dan leaned forward, elbows on his knees and lowered his voice, "food and water need to be stocked up as fast as you can. Next is whatever weapons you can find. Then you got to have a way to keep them out. Your fence is up and that's about your only saving grace. We're lucky in the country here. We aren't going to face the mobs of those monsters like in the city."

"Don't be ridiculous," I snapped, fear making me surly. "There isn't going to be any horde or pack or whatever you think there's going to be." A breeze blew in and I spun to close the door. I gasped at the sight of the person standing on the edge of the doorstep. Missy leapt to her feet and let out a long low growl, followed by a sharp bark. I grabbed her collar, holding her back.

I vaguely recognized him as the portly clerk from Tom's Grocery. But he was no longer chubby. He was lean, with the excess flesh hanging off his arms and face. His skin was a sickly yellow like the man on the TV--the man that had attacked the reporter. Worst was the way his pupils had become a horizontal slit of animalism that stole his humanity.

"Hungry," was all he said as he launched himself

at me. I stumbled backwards, letting go of Missy as I fell. With a grunt, I struck out with my knife and got nothing but air. We hit the ground and I rolled, trying to remember my distant Judo lessons, failing miserably. Missy latched onto his ankle and was doing her damnedest to yank him off me. He didn't even look at her, like he didn't feel her teeth buried in his leg.

The clerk ended up on top of me but he didn't pin my knife hand; I suppose he was too focused on taking a bite out of me. Before I knew what I was doing, I had my left hand wrapped around his throat to keep his snapping teeth off me, and I slammed the knife upwards into his heart. Blood spurted out around the blade and down the handle, warm with the last of his life.

As suddenly as it happened, it was over. The clerk was yanked off me and Sebastian stared down at me with a look of horror across his face. Dan stepped up next to him. "She's got a good survival instinct. That'll serve you well. If she were a screamer, you'd be dead in no time. Good dog, too. Should have thought of that before."

Missy hurried to me and licked my face a couple of times. I didn't push her away.

I lay on the floor staring up at Sebastian and Dan as my brain tried to process what happened. I'd been attacked, and I'd killed a man. In less time than it took to take a breath, my life had twisted itself inside out. My hands were slick with his blood, and as I stood, a wave of vertigo washed over me.

"She's gonna puke."

Hands were on me, guiding me outside where I did indeed puke, heaving 'til my stomach was empty and sweat beaded on my forehead from the dry heaves. Dan turned the hose on and I washed my hands clean and sprayed the cool water over my face. I had killed a man. My stomach clenched again and I dry heaved again.

"Oh shit," Sebastian said, his voice off to my right, his hands tightening on my arms.

"I'll be okay," I said.

"Not you, babe," he turned me to the front of our property and the open gate, "them."

Maybe it wasn't a horde, but there was close to twenty people walking our way. Their heads wove a little from side to side, as if they were listening for something, and their hands twitched and clenched over and over again. The distinct yellow of their skin visible even from that distance.

A thought hit me. "If they're so damn hungry, why aren't they eating each other?" I clutched at Sebastian's hand.

Dan grunted. "You don't eat other predators unless you have to. Predators eat prey, girl."

Prey. . . we were the prey.

Sebastian let me go and ran for the gate. Missy bolted alongside him.

"Bastian, don't!" I yelled and as a unit, every one of the Nevermore's heads snapped up, and their goat-slit eyes focused on the source of the scream.

Me.

"Damn it, girl, I told you no noise," Dan growled

as he walked past me to the edge of the deck and put his gun to his shoulder. Lifting it, he rested it on the railing and took aim at the running horde. There was a soft pop, and the Nevermore at the front of the pack dropped. I slapped my hands over my mouth.

Dan's shot gave Sebastian time to reach the gate ahead of the first Nevermores. He grabbed the left-hand side and slammed it shut. Missy shot out and yanked the legs out from under the Nevermore next closest to Sebastian.

Oh God. How could this all be happening? It couldn't be real. This was some sort of nightmare.

Sebastian reached out, grabbed Missy by the collar and yanked her into the yard. The Nevermore, released from her bite lurched forward. Sebastian dropped him with a punch to the nose, grabbed the second panel of the gate and slammed it shut.

The Nevermores hit the gate hard, shuddering the frame. They hammered their bodies against it, screaming and howling, their eyes wild as they reached through the bars for Sebastian.

I ran down the steps of the porch, jumped across the flowerbeds, and raced to where Sebastian stood panting. He bent over with his hands braced on his thighs, staring at the horde in front of us.

"Why aren't they trying to climb the gate?" I whispered.

Sebastian shook his head, breathing hard. "The TV talked about. . . loss of motor skills. It might save us."

That had been a quick sprint for a man of his size, faster than I'd seen him move in years.

Dan strolled up next to us, casually, like he was out for a Sunday visit. Except for the gun slung over his shoulder and the horde of Nevermores at our gate, he could have been doing just that.

"Interesting, that. They don't seem to be able to figure it out. Like animals penned up."

But even as he spoke, one of the Nevermores pushed his way through to the front of the group and began to fiddle with the gate, his fingers clumsy and far from dexterous. He didn't seem able to use the finer movements of motor skills, which was better for us. "Looks like you were right, Bastian. I don't remember that bit, but I could have missed it."

"What bit?" Dan asked.

"Sebastian said he saw a piece about the Nevermores losing their dexterity, all their fine motor skills."

Dan shot a look at Bastian. "I didn't see anything about that."

Sebastian shrugged, and looked away from Dan. "You must have missed it."

There was a moment of tense silence and then the rattle of the gate and a low growl from Missy broke it.

The Nevermore at the gate fiddled with the locking mechanism and Missy leapt at him, snapping her teeth. We were in trouble if the Nevermores figured out how to open it. Real trouble.

And I had a feeling it was only a matter of time.

"We've got to get out of here. They aren't going to

give up as long as they can see a smorgasbord on this side of the gate." Sebastian pulled me with him as he backed away. I didn't need a lot of encouragement—he was right, out of sight could be out of mind for the monsters. I was not interested in facing down that horde anytime soon. Thank God our place was fully fenced.

We retreated to the house, around the corner out of sight of the gate. "We're stuck here for a while, boy." Dan chewed his cigar, rolling it around with his lips. "Might as well get used to the idea, unless you've got an army tank in that shed over there." Dan pointed to the dilapidated chicken coop we'd partially knocked down in preparation for a garden.

It was only then I realized Sebastian hadn't meant that we should just get out of sight, but off our property completely.

I pursed my lips, thinking. Sebastian could be right. It might be better to go somewhere we weren't out in the middle of nowhere. Then again, Dan had said something about the city being worse than rural because of the number of people.

"We don't need a tank," I surprised myself by speaking my thoughts out loud to a virtual stranger. "We'll just take the car. They can't stop us, and if they try, we'll just run them over."

I could barely believe the words that came out of my mouth and apparently neither could Sebastian.

"You're kidding, right? Those things out there are people underneath it all, and you want to run them over? The TV said they were working on an antidote. They aren't hurting us right now. So we won't hurt them. That's pretty much murder if we go out there and randomly start mowing them down."

I sucked in a sharp breath and he flinched as though I'd hit him. I'd just killed a man, a Nevermore because he attacked me. Did Sebastian think I was a murderer then?

"In case you haven't noticed, they want to eat us, not play Parcheesi," I put my hands on my hips as flush of embarrassment and horror shot through me. "And I think if we are defending ourselves, that's a hell of a lot different than murder."

A sharp rattle snapped all three of our heads toward the gate in unison. The horde leaned into the steel gates, and the hinges groaned. Every last one of them had their mouths open, teeth showing with their lips pulled back, saliva dripping and hanging from them. How long would the gates hold? A week? A day?

An hour?

"We need to get farther out of sight," Dan said, walking toward the porch on the far side of the house.

"I think Sebastian is right. We need to get out of here before more of those things show up." I said, hysteria bubbling up. I'd just killed a man and we had a horde of drug-induced-use-to-be-human-monsters on our doorstep. I clapped my hands over my face and tried to block out the moment. The sights were gone, but the groan of the gates, the growling of the hoard still reached me, denying me my moment of escape. A part of my brain tried to tell me I was being irrational, that I wasn't really making any sense.

The other part said to run as far and fast as I could.

A hand on my arm snapped my eyes open. Sebastian dragged me toward the house. Not because he wasn't trying to be gentle, but because I couldn't seem to get my legs to work.

"We'll talk about what we're going to do inside. The last thing we need is to go off half-cocked and get ourselves killed, okay, babe?"

I let him direct my body, but I couldn't help but stare over my shoulder at the writhing mass of limbs and snapping mouths that had, until very recently, been human. "This can't be happening."

A sharp shake brought my eyes up to Sebastian. Fear and the denial of that fear made his eyes those of a person I barely recognized.

"It is happening, Mara, and you need to get used to the idea because we have to figure out what we're going to do," he said, his mouth a thin hard line.

I jerked my arm out of his hands, anger superseding the fear.

"You're an ass, you know that, don't you?" I said as I stomped toward the front door, slamming it behind me. All I wanted was a little comfort, a white lie or two to get through the initial shock. After that, I could come to terms with what was going on—I'd done it twice before. Both times I believed the lies that I could get pregnant again, that we could have a family. Those lies had been enough to get me through the hardest part of the grief.

The living room was dim with only the flickering of the TV for light. The curtains and blinds were drawn down. Dan sat on the couch, his feet propped up on the hand-carved coffee table that Bastian's Gran had given us as a wedding gift.

"Feet off," I said, shoving his boots to the floor before he could remove them himself. "I don't care if this is the end of the world, I don't want your feet on my damn coffee table."

The door opened behind me and shut with a soft click. I kept my back turned to Sebastian. My spine was rigid and my inhale and exhale were slow and deliberate as I tried to rein in my anger.

Missy scratched at the bathroom door with a low whine. I strode down the hallway and swung the door open. Nero tried to scamper between my legs but I scooped him up and held him tightly at the same time pressing a hand to Missy's head. She pressed herself against my hand and some of the anger drained out of me. Taking one last deep breath, I carried Nero into the living room, Missy tightly by my side.

My feet came to a sudden stop as the image on the TV flickered. I stared, unable to take my eyes off the screen.

Dan leaned forward from his spot on the couch. "I'd hoped they'd have gotten it under control in the bigger cities at least. They said they were bringing in the army."

I slid into an empty chair, my legs suddenly numb. "I don't think that's the case." My hands trembled as I stroked Nero, and Missy sat at my side, her chin on my knee.

The screen was simple, black and white with a flashing red pulse behind it. Simple, and so, so horrifying.

The announcer's voice came on, apparently in a loop. "These are the major cities that have been overrun and are considered uninhabitable. This is no particular order: Toronto, Vancouver, Seattle, San Francisco, Los Angeles, Edmonton, Brisbane, New York, Atlanta, Ottawa, London, Perth, Paris, Frankfurt, Berlin, Glasgow, Mexico City, Venice, Lima . . ."

The list went on and on, scrolling for a solid two minutes before it broke.

"Every continent has been hit by this catastrophe, though some obviously worse than others." The male announcer's voice blared louder than before, almost like he shouted into the microphone. I jumped involuntarily, gasping for air. Missy pressed her chin against my leg harder, as if to press me back into my seat. Shaking, I gave her a pat and put Nero in my lap so they were close together.

The camera panned to a reporter wearing a rumpled blue suit. His hair was not slicked back, but looked as if he'd been running his hands through it, over and over. Subsequently, every strand seemed to be standing on end. He stood in a rather bare-bones room, cement walls, and shelves of strange scientific-looking paraphernalia. Microscopes, vials, lab coats, and many instruments I had no names for.

"Bruce Gunder, here, reporting from Dr. Josephson's lab. Dr. Josephson is a virologist based in Vancouver, British Columbia. Dr. Josephson, what can you tell us about the current events of the world? Will the Nevermore drug wear off? What can we do about this situation while the government gathers itself to deal with it?" Bruce turned to the camera every few words as if to gain permission from the viewing audience to ask the questions.

"It's simple, even for a nincompoop like you, Blaine," Dr. Josephson said.

"It's Bruce, actually."

The scientist shook his head. "Whatever. The drug was tested thoroughly. But because of the high demand, the processing became . . . well, let's call it careless. The toxins from cystius scoparius were not completely removed as they were during the initial trials." He drew a breath and shook his head again. "You can imagine, though, that the companies behind it didn't really care. Money makes the world go 'round, and Nevermore has been bringing in a shit ton of money."

"Can he say that on TV?" Sebastian asked and Dan whacked him on the shoulder.

"Shut up."

Dr. Josephson continued. "In the two months since the production ramped up and the fail-safe checks faltered, I calculate conservatively that it has made over one point six trillion dollars. You can imagine how that would make a company eager to turn a blind eye to a few minor details. Like missing a single screening process which ups their profit margin by an additional thirty percent."

Bruce leaned in. "Those numbers can't be right."

Dr. Josephson snorted. "Three hundred thirty-seven million people, give or take a few thousand, get the shot through legal means. That's in North America alone. Five thousand dollars a shot, one hundred people a day per clinic. You should do your research before you go on air, Bruno.

"I know the details because I was one of the scientists working on developing the drug. I oversaw the processing, helped to weed out the issues with the main component. The company wouldn't listen to me when I brought the issue to their attention. They fired me for warning them."

Bruce leaned back in his seat. "You . . . this isn't speculation."

"No, Brutus, it isn't. I was there on the front lines. I saw it happening. I tried to warn them."

The doctor sat on a ratty old stool and looked into the camera as if Bruce were no longer worth speaking to.

"I want to make something very clear to the public. There is no cure. There is no chance it will go away. It won't wear off, it is designed to link permanently to the molecular structure of human bones, organs, and most importantly, the brain. It cannot be transferred by a bite as the modern movie culture would have you believe.

"These are not zombies from some B-Grade

movie franchise. These are people—humans— who have gone feral, wild. They have returned to a more basic structure of existence. You have a time period of about six weeks from the time the shot is given to when the transition is complete. So expect that over the next two months to see an increase in the numbers of Nevermores."

"Holy shit." Bruce shoved himself in front of the doctor but Josephson was having none of it. He grabbed the edge of the camera and pulled it close. "These Nevermores, they are acting as packs, not unlike a pack of wolves with an Alpha male and female with the rest working as a group for food and protection. They are far more sophisticated than we first realized. They have forms of communicating I'm not sure we will be able to understand given the time we have left." His pale blue eyes seemed to bore into me and I shivered with the intensity. "So, to the few people who have not taken Nevermore, I will say only one thing more." He paused, dropped his head and shook it slightly before looking back up into the camera.

"Find a way to survive."

CHAPTER ELEVEN

Sebastian

The entire time the TV announcer was speaking . . . it was like I was standing back and watching a movie. Because . . . there was no way I was becoming one of those . . .monsters.

I sat there, feeling the burn in my thigh from where the needle had gone in. Feeling the tingle through my muscles and blood as my adrenaline shifted into high gear. It took all of my control to keep my breath from not coming out in gasps and gulps. I'd never had a panic attack, but I was pretty sure I was on the cusp of one. The edges of my vision were tinged in sparkles and darkness as I stared at the TV, watched the reporter and scientist talk. I heard the words, but at the same time, I couldn't stop the way my mind raced to other things.

Like knowing that the Nevermore's dexterity was dull at best.

Because I'd seen it in my head when I'd shut the gate. I'd seen the frustration of the Nevermore in front of me, seen an image in my head of him wanting the gate open, but being unable to do it. Unable to make his fingers work right.

But that wasn't possible.

Unless . . . unless that was how they communicated.

My stomach rolled and I almost puked my guts out. I swallowed the rising gorge and clenched my hands on my thighs.

Maybe . . . I hadn't taken the whole shot . . . hope bloomed for a second. That could be good. Maybe it wouldn't affect me the same way, or maybe I could keep it at bay longer. I realized then that was my only hope.

Earlier in the day, I'd gone into the city directly to the police station to tell them about the farm incident where I'd gotten Missy and Nero. The city had been weirdly quiet, except for the grocery store and the police station which seemed to be the two epicenters of chaos.

I'd bypassed the grocery store, even though I should have seen that as a sign. I realized that now. But at the time, I went right to the police station.

There was shouting and the sound of guns going off. People had been all over the lawn. Some of the police officers had been fighting their own people. Police against police. Only some were yellow skinned and the others were still human.

I'd run for my car and driven all the way home in a dead panic.

Because I'd seen the thoughts of the Nevermore's fighting the police. The insatiable hunger that had been driving them to attack their previous co-workers and friends. I'd seen what they planned. The first bite going for the throat or hamstring, the second and third straight for the soft underbelly.

Worse was the saliva that had filled my own mouth.

Terror had driven me.

And then I was home.

And the TV.

And the words.

And my new reality.

I was going to be one of the monsters sooner or later. More likely sooner by the sounds of it. A fine tremor started up in my spine, somewhere in the middle of the scientist's speech. I would try and hurt Mara, try and eat her.

No. I refused to believe I could fall to that. Refused to believe I would become that monster. I loved her too much to hurt her.

Didn't I?

CHAPTER TWELVE

Mara

The TV went blank and the screen turned into a warning system of striped colors. The silence in our home was overwhelming and I wanted to say something to break it. I couldn't think of anything that would mean anything, and since screaming hysterically was out of the question, I was out of options.

Dan stood, drawing our attention. "That's it, then. I'm headed back to my place."

"What?" Sebastian stood with him. "You can't get out of here alive. There's no way you'll make it all the way back to your place past those . . . Nevermores." He seemed to choke on that last word.

Dan strolled to the back door, ignoring Sebastian's assessment. He glanced over his shoulder at us. "There's a back trail from the south side of your property. It goes up and around through the bush, skirting most of the properties. It's got a great view of the ocean at the top. I think these things . . ."

"Nevermores," I said softly.

Dan nodded at me. "These Nevermores seem to be sticking to the main routes, right now. They'll find the trails soon enough, just like any predator, and use it for travel and hunting. For now, if you come to my place, come the back way. I'll put a red flag next to it. Other than that, plant a garden, grow yourself some food, mend your fences, and keep the noise down."

He put his hand on the door and I leapt up to grab the back of his grubby shirt.

"Hey, you can't just leave us here. I thought you were our friend." Okay, I thought he was Sebastian's friend. But that was beside the point.

Dan laughed and half turned back to me. "You city folk are going to be the first to die off—you aren't prepared, and despite what I said earlier, I doubt you have any real survival instinct." His eyes narrowed as he looked at me, as if weighing me. "You might make it for a time; you got some good reflexes on you. If you survive the first month, you could last."

Sebastian stepped up behind me, but said nothing. I didn't let go of Dan. "You could help us. You've already been helping Sebastian a bit, right? At least we could be working together. Numbers could help us. None of us got the shot. We should be working together," I said.

Dan laughed again. "I don't work with anybody. It ain't my style. Too much drama when you get more than one person in a room."

"So," Sebastian said, "we're supposed to be grateful you showed up for a belated house warming, and you didn't even bring us a gift? You happen to visit in the middle of a crisis where you don't even help? I don't know why you bothered at all."

I let go of Dan's coat, feeling my own anger build. What the hell was Dan's reasoning, or was he truly just as crazy as we'd heard?

Dan straightened his coat and lifted an eyebrow at us then nodded slowly. "All right, I got a deal for you. If you can make it to my place, I'll let you have a—as in singular—weapon. But I'm telling you this now, this whole shit show that is happening, it might be a man-made crisis. But this is Mother Nature's way of weeding out the weak. Only the strong and savvy will survive this, and that's how it should be." He paused and grinned at us. "To tell you the truth, I came here to take what you had and add it to my stores. But you were still here, still alive. I'm curious to see how long you last now. Might be my only form of entertainment for a while."

I stared at him in disbelief, the reality of the situation hitting me hard, right in the center of my chest like a punch.

The door clicked softly as he left. I was not surprised that he didn't say goodbye or good luck. That wasn't his style.

"Well, that was . . .unpleasant," Sebastian said. "He's right, though. You could survive this, you've got the steel in your spine. It's what made you a good business woman."

I stared at my husband. He was rambling.

Had Dan meant for us to mend our fences around the property, or the proverbial ones between Sebastian and me? I doubted Dan was that insightful, but his words reverberated in my head. I took in Bastian's drawn face and worried eyes, and the way his pulse jumped in the hollow of his throat. He was holding it together, but underneath that control, he was as scared as I was. Forgiveness flowed through me. My heart gave a thump and I all but threw myself into Sebastian's arms.

Between sobs and begging for forgiveness on both sides, our lips met and we caught the edge of a mania that perhaps other survivors were feeling. My mom had always said there was a reason for baby booms every generation. It had to do with people wanting to feel alive in the midst of terror. People wanted to live while they had a chance.

We stripped each other out of our clothes, piece by piece, consumed by the need to touch one another. Leaving the dogs downstairs, we stumbled up to the second floor bathroom. The water still ran. We hadn't lost power, though, I suppose it would happen at some point. I was covered in flecks of blood and dirt. The hot water tank barely held up for the amount of time we stayed under the water, showering off the sweat and remnants of blood. Wrapped around each other, I knew that as long as I had Bastian, I could do this. I could face anything with him at my side. For a few moments, we were safe in our tiny house in the middle of nowhere. We had each other, and that would be enough. The fear mixed in with the love we clung to as we wrapped around one another and washed the darkness away for a moment or two.

We made love in the shower and then again in the bedroom which was unlike either of us. Sebastian was usually done in after one round. But our frantic need to touch and feel overwhelmed any common sense or past stamina issues.

The problem was it had stopped us from thinking straight. Maybe Dan was right, maybe we wouldn't survive because we were too dumb to think about something rather simple—like locking the doors.

To be fair, though, we hadn't locked our doors since moving to the country. It just wasn't done when neighbors lived as far apart as we did.

Lying in each other's arms, we dozed off. I wanted to believe this was all a dream, a nightmare come to life in the night. But by the morning, the light of day would shatter the darkness and fear.

Not so much.

From the first floor, Missy let out a woof. I sat up in bed and stared at the dark walls.

"Bastian. Someone is in the house."

He lurched up and rubbed at his face. "It's Jessica."

I turned and stared at him. "How do you know that?"

The bedroom door creaked, the knob clicked against something, perhaps nails.

Chills rippled over my body, the sensation of being watched heightened by the darkness and shadows of the room.

"Bastian, you don't know it's her," I whispered, my eyes picking out a figure silhouetted in the doorway. Slim, for sure, but there was no way he could know it was Jessica.

"It is," he grunted, swinging his legs to one side of the bed.

I wasn't convinced. Keeping as still as possible, I franticly searched the room with my eyes, seeking a weapon of any sort.

"Help me." Her voice was raspy, but I recognized it right away. How had Sebastian known, though?

I jumped up out of bed. "Jessica?"

"Help me, please," her body twitched and she kept her arms wrapped around her middle. I flicked on the overhead light and Sebastian cursed.

"We're naked here, babe," he said as he yanked on clothes. I did the same, keeping an eye on Jessica the whole time. Her Caribbean blue eyes were semi-glazed and she didn't seem to realize we were naked. Okay, she didn't look at me. She may have glanced more than once at Sebastian, but I didn't care, and he didn't seem to notice. Thank goodness for small blessings.

"Honey," I said slipping a T-shirt over my head, "your parents, where are they?"

"Gone, they turned into monsters and I . . . they just ignored me and they ran out of the house," she whispered and clutched at her body harder.

I froze in mid-motion of pulling my shirt over my head.

"Shit." I yanked my shirt the rest of the way on. "Why didn't they try to attack her?"

"My thoughts exactly, wife."

I moved toward Jessica and wondered again why she had taken Nevermore. Thin as a rail, pretty, and yet she'd had the shot, as had her mother and father. Her blue eyes were still human, still with a perfect round iris. They'd not yet slid into the realm of the feral horde outside our front gate. How long would it be before they turned color and she became one of the monsters?

I touched her arm and she flinched. "It's okay. Let's go downstairs and see what we can do."

"The TV said there isn't a cure, that it won't wear off. I don't want to be a monster," she said, her voice breaking with a sob. Gone was the over-confident teenager I'd gone on a walk with earlier. Had it really only been hours before? It felt like a lifetime had passed since then.

I nodded. "I know, but that could change. I'm sure they're working on a cure, right now. They said that on the TV, too, you know."

Sebastian made a rude noise and I shushed him. I knew when to tell a white lie. This was a teenage girl who was terrified and alone; the least I could do was try and comfort her. Even if it was false, it was a kindness.

Once downstairs and seated at the kitchen table with a hot tea in front of her, Jessica told us what happened.

"Parkinson's runs strong in our family on both sides. I . . .had some tremors here and there already. So my parents wanted to make sure I never had to deal with it. They insisted I take the shot with them. I saw you at the clinic when my mom took me in to get it."

I leaned forward and put my hand over hers. It took some effort not to flinch as she twitched underneath my fingers, but I wanted her to be calm so she would keep talking. "And it was today that your parent's turned?"

"Only an hour ago," she whispered as she stared into her tea. "I don't have very long, do I?"

Tears welled up in my eyes and I blinked them back. I didn't know Jessica well, but it was hard to see someone so young cut down by something that should have helped her live a long and healthy life. It was hard knowing there was really nothing we could do to help.

Missy and Nero sat by the stove and when Nero moved to come closer, Missy stopped him, directing him to me. I stood and fixed them a big bowl of food. Missy spun in circles while I tore open the bag of dog food Sebastian got for them. I felt bad for ignoring them, but they wagged their tails in unison and seemed to have forgiven me already.

I put the bowl on the floor and they jumped on it. Missy had warned us of an intruder. That was worth more than a bowl of food.

"How long ago did your parents take the shot?" Sebastian asked, leaning toward her.

"Five weeks; I was a week later. But the TV said it was closer to six weeks before people turned." Her eyes flicked up to him twice, maybe intimidated by his size, the way a lot of people were. Then I remembered she had a crush on him. I could only imagine the embarrassment of finding her crush in bed naked with his wife.

Sebastian stood up so quickly, his chair screeched out behind him. Missy, Nero, and I jumped, but Jessica didn't move. Bastian stomped out of the house. I frowned after him. "Bastian?"

He waved a hand in the air like that explained it all. What was going on in his head?

I ignored him, knowing Jessica needed comfort right now more than he needed calming. "You can stay here, sweetheart. It'll be okay." Then I frowned. "How did you make it past the horde out front?"

She gave me a wobbly, tear filled smile. "They know I'm one of them, same as my parents. They let me pass, I climbed the gate and they," she shrugged, "there's no other way to say it, they cheered for me, like they were happy I could get in here to you." Dropping her head to her arms on the table she let out a sob. I reached over and put a hand on her head, fighting with my own rising emotions: sadness, fear, and then relief. It could have been me waiting to be turned into an animal. If not for the damn Scotch broom it would be me.

I would have taken the shot in an instant. Funny how life turned out, how it changed in a split second of decisions taken out of your control. A curse into a blessing.

I ushered Jessica to the back bedroom and tucked her into bed, giving her three anti-histamines. They always made me groggy, so they should knock her out for the rest of the night. "Just call, if you need anything."

"Thanks," she said softly, then yawned. "You're really nice. Maybe nice enough."

I raised my eyebrows. What did she mean by that? Or were the drugs already kicking in? That was possible, they always made me loopy. I rubbed a hand under my neck. Speaking of the anti-histamines . . .I went out to the kitchen and took one myself. Not to help with sleep, but for the reaction I was having to some airborne allergen. Lucky me and my hay fever.

All over my body, my skin tingled in circular patches. My chest, belly, neck and around my mouth, as well as my inner thighs which was a weird spot even for me. My eyes watered, and the back of my throat itched, sure signs I'd gotten hit with something my body didn't like.

The next task was to see what was going on with Sebastian. Nero and Missy followed me onto the back porch. My earlier fear at the situation we'd found ourselves in slowly turned into resolve. Despite what Dan said, I knew we could survive whatever was thrown at us. We were smart, young, and in love. There wasn't anything we couldn't do.

Bastian was on the back porch, leaning against the railing, staring out at the star encrusted black sky. I stepped beside him and slipped my arm around his waist.

"I haven't had the chance yet to thank you," I said.

He gave me a quizzical look and I pointed at the two dogs sitting next to me. To be fair, Nero sat on my foot, his mom beside me. I smiled, "You didn't have to get me a puppy, but I'm glad you did. And I'm glad you brought Missy along, too." I gave his waist a squeeze and took a deep breath, letting it out slowly.

"I couldn't leave her there; she would have died."

I nodded. "I know."

We were quiet for a moment, just standing, staring at the property that was supposed to be our dream home. The place we stayed forever. The sound of crickets and an owl hooted now and then. There was no sound of monsters at the gate. Nothing that gave away the situation we were in.

Time to make our plan. "We've got to lay out what we are going to do, Bastian. Food, water, fences, weapons. Maybe get some sort of radio up in case there are notices once the electricity is out," I said. I looked up and my breath caught in my throat. Tears streaked his face, dripped off his chin and plunked onto the railing.

He wrapped his arms around me. "It isn't fair, Mara. That girl in there is losing everything because she wanted to have a life. Because her family didn't want her to suffer with a disease she had no say on contracting in the first place." His voice was thick with emotion and I held onto him as tightly as I could as I fought my own tears. To say I was shocked at what I was seeing was an understatement. Sebastian was usually so stoic. In four years, this was perhaps the second time I'd seen him shed tears—and the first time I wasn't entirely certain it wasn't just a hard wind causing his eyes to water.

His mom had told me he'd never even cried at the funeral for his dad and brother. He'd just stood looking sad, but not a single tear.

"Go to bed, babe. I'll stay up and watch over you two. I don't think I could sleep anyway."

I kissed him softly on his lips, holding his head in my hands. "I love you, Bastian, more than anything."

He kissed me back and swatted me lightly on my butt as I turned to go inside.

I went upstairs to bed, taking Missy and Nero with me. I took Missy to the bathroom first and made sure the bite wounds in her back were clean, then smothered them in an antibiotic ointment I had stashed in the cupboard. Satisfied I'd done what I could, I snapped my fingers and she followed me into the bedroom, Nero trailing behind. I scooped him up and Missy leapt onto the bed without being asked. I laughed.

"Think you own the place now, do you?"

She panted with her tongue hanging out with what looked like a saucy grin to me and flopped onto the bed with her head on her paws. I snuggled Nero down in with me and Missy scooted so she could lay across my legs.

From below us came the sound of Sebastian pacing on the porch. From time to time, he muttered, but I couldn't make out the words.

My mind whirled with plans as to what we could

do to make it through this new world. In my head, I sketched out the best place for a garden—the current spot was far too rocky—where the fence needed to be reinforced, and what we could use as weapons besides the knives we had. I wasn't sure we'd try to get to Dan's place for a weapon. That is if he'd even give us one if we made the effort.

I yawned and closed my eyes, the two dogs snuggling in tightly to me. Their steady warmth and soft sound of their breathing were a steady comfort. Sometime just before dawn, I finally drifted off to sleep.

CHAPTER THIRTEEN

Sebastian

The cool night air didn't ease the sweat that prickled on my skin from every pore. I'd sent Mara away because I couldn't tell her the truth. I wasn't crying for Jessica.

I was crying for me and Mara.

I scrubbed at my face as I paced the porch, back and forth. "What are you going to do?" I asked myself the question, not really expecting an answer.

"You could come with me."

I spun around. Jessica stood on the edge of the doorway. She shut the door behind her and wobbled toward me. I caught her before she could fall and she leaned into me. I pushed her toward one of the chairs and glanced up at the second floor.

"Go back to bed, kid." I kept my words low. I'd seen inside Jessica's head clearly when she'd stumbled into our bedroom earlier.

She hadn't been bothered by the nudity ... if anything, it had excited her. The sobbing and breath catching had all been an act. A very, very good act.

My jaw clenched, anger building in me. "Mara is my wife. That isn't going to change."

Jessica shivered. "I see your anger in my head. I believe you."

I took a step back. "What do you mean?"

She shrugged and the blanket she'd wrapped herself in slid down her shoulders revealing more than a little bare skin. "I can feel it, on my skin. I know you're angry with me. I saw you looking at me in the bedroom, irritated."

An image flickered through my mind of Jessica on top of me, my hands on her breasts as she rode me. I gasped and took a step back. "You don't really think that's going to happen, do you?"

"I think you're just like me. We . . . are not going to be here much longer. Which means we could be together."

She smiled and I realized she was completely serious. "Daddy issues much?"

Her smile slipped, and her lips turned into a grimace. "No."

I kept my pacing to the far side of the deck. I could have tried to forcibly move her away, could have tried to make her go back to bed, but that would have required touching her and even I knew that was a bad idea.

"Go back to bed."

"Come with me."

I glared at her. I no longer doubted Dan's words of caution about her. Though I wished she'd thought to go somewhere else when her parents turned. The thought rumbled out in a question. "How long ago did your parent's really turn?"

She shrugged. "A few days ago. Doesn't really matter does it?"

All of it was an act, I'd known it. Caught glimpses of it in the images that floated from her to me. But it was if . . . "You know how to keep things from me already?"

Her grin was pure undiluted pleasure. "Yes, I've been practicing. My parents thought I wasn't going to be one of the monsters, that I got a better batch than them."

Holy shit. "How?"

"Kiss me and I'll teach you." She stood and let the blanket drop to the floor. Unsurprisingly she was completely naked. I scoffed.

"I'm not a horny teenager. Get away from me. I'll figure it out myself."

"Don't you want to touch me?"

I'd had enough of this shit. "Not with a ten-foot pole would I touch your skanky prepubescent body. Not if you were the last girl on the planet."

She sucked in a sharp breath and her eyes flashed with anger. With a quick spin, she raced into the house. She grabbed the door and swung it backward and I leapt forward, catching the edge of it. The last thing I wanted was for Mara to be woken.

"You're lucky I don't scream."

"You're lucky I don't throw you off the property," I snarled, feeling a rage that had never made itself known to me. We locked eyes and that rage grew and she shrunk from it.

Alpha. The word rippled in my mind, and she bobbed her head and backed away from me quietly.

Breathing hard, I watched until she shut the bedroom door.

My wife was a softie and she wanted to help Jessica so I would play along for now. More than anything, I didn't want to upset Mara more than I had to. I didn't want to add to her stress.

And maybe I could learn a thing or two from the kid about hiding thoughts. If nothing else, she was an amazing actress. I would need to hide stuff from Mara, at least for a little while.

I went back to the porch and put both hands on the railing and leaned out, breathing in the night. I had to calm myself. Slowly the anger drained, and I was able to count my heart beats as separate pulses instead of an uneven staccato.

An image flickered through my brain. Our wrought iron gate, fingers reaching through, a scent curling through me, remembering food on this side. I stepped off the porch and headed around the side of the house.

At the gate were two Nevermores. They fumbled quietly with the latch, as though they could figure it out. Or maybe they recalled when they could manage something as simple as a lock.

They glanced up at me but didn't seem bothered

by my presence. I kept moving closer and closer until I was right at the gate looking out at them.

I crouched in front of them and watched them. Their fingers didn't bend the right way. They seemed to be able to curl, but they couldn't bring their thumb to any of their fingers. It was almost as if they couldn't truly feel where their own hands were.

The tingles that I'd first experienced from the shot suddenly raced down my arms into my fingers and the tips went numb. Numb.

I scrambled backward, falling onto my ass, I moved so fast. The two Nevermores grunted at me, one of them reached forward and beckoned me to come closer. I couldn't seem to help myself. I moved, shuffling forward, and I reached through the fence. To their side.

The one who'd called me sniffed my hand all over and grunted, then put his cheek against my palm. I knew, though I didn't know how I knew.

Submission. He was submitting to me. The other one tipped his head and sniffed the air. He tried to grasp the bar of the gate but couldn't get a grip. So they couldn't climb either. Or at least, they couldn't for now.

There was a barking scream in the distance and they both spun, staring down the road. They took one last look at me and bolted away. But not before I saw the image of what scared them.

The Beta in the pack, a male that took to biting the others and beating them badly when they stepped out of line. He was not as big as me, but bulky with muscles that were clearly defined. I closed my eyes but the image stayed.

The thing was, I was sure I'd met him before he was turned . . . in fact the angle of his jaw, the tilt of his eyes . . .I was sure his daughter slept in our back bedroom.

CHAPTER FOURTEEN

Mara

Dreams haunted what I'd hope would be a restful sleep. They left me wishing I'd stayed up with Sebastian. Sleep deprivation would have been better than what I'd tossed and turned with all night.

Over and over, the clerk attacked me again, but this time I was on my own. Sebastian lay in a pool of blood beside me. Dan was nowhere to be found. Missy was pinned to the wall with giant push pins like an oversized bug, and Nero barked madly around my feet. My belly was distended with growing life, only it wasn't a human child, but a Nevermores. The baby clawed at my insides, trying to break free. I put a hand on my belly. "I'm your momma. Let me love you." And my belly went quiet. When the clerk attacked me and I realized I was with child, I snapped. A mother bear's ferocity roared out from a place within me I never knew existed.

The clerk never had a chance as he leapt at me. I swept the knife up and pierced his heart in a single blow. His strange eyes glazed over as death settled on him and he slumped to the floor in a puddle of blood next to Sebastian. But there was no time to grieve. A boom from the other side of the house rattled through the air, and the back porch door flung open. A wave of Nevermores poured in. They wore the faces of my family and friends: Sebastian's Gran, my mom, my best friend Amy . . . but they were coming for me with blood lust in their eyes. I yanked my blade out of the clerk's chest, and reached for the front door. I had to get away. I pulled on the handle of the door. It was locked and my hand slid over the mechanism to unlock it, over and over, unable to grasp it as though my hands were those of a Nevermore's.

I screamed and turned back to the horde. They rushed me and I fought like a mad woman, protecting the child within me even while it resumed its efforts to get out. I blocked hands and mouths, sliced off fingers and stabbed at eyes. Nero barked and bit, but his little body was flung aside like a rag doll, and he disappeared into the maw of one of the Nevermores. The horde howled and swelled, slammed me to the ground, pinned me as they shook me.

I screamed, or tried to, and a hand covered my mouth.

"You're dreaming, babe. It's just a dream. You're okay." Sebastian's deep rumble in my ear slowed my heart rate as I came fully awake. A dream, it had only been a dream. But it had felt so real, so . . . possible.

I hated nightmares like that the most, the ones that could actually happen. I smoothed a hand over my face, pushing Bastian's hand off my mouth.

"What time is it?"

"What?"

"Time? We've got a lot to do." Better that I focus on the things I could control.

"It's just after seven. Jessica's still asleep."

I got up, still in my clothes from the day before when Jessica had woken us so suddenly. "I guess I should shower." I plucked at my T-shirt.

"Might as well, at some point we're going to lose electricity, and then no more hot showers or washing machine." He kissed me on the cheek, bent and scooped up a yawning Nero. "I'm going to make breakfast for us and the little man here and his momma." He ruffled the puppy's hair and disappeared into the hallway. Missy, though, stayed with me.

"Go on, you want to eat don't you?" I shooed her off the bed, but she took her time. I wondered if the bites on her back were bothering her and gave them a look. They weren't infected or anything and seemed to be healing. Still, she was reluctant to leave me. I had to walk her to the top of the stairs before she'd go.

Her loyalty in such a short time was nothing short of amazing. Then again, Sebastian had rescued her. That had to have earned us some brownie points with her.

I showered, taking my time in the hot water. It was hard to imagine being without the simple parts of life, the day-to-day luxuries. It looked like we were about to embark on the camping trip from hell that wouldn't ever end. Not really the most pleasant of thoughts for a newly relocated city girl. No. I had to have faith in those who were in charge. There had been more than one news anchor who'd said there was a cure being sought, that the army was involved.

So we would just hunker down and wait this out. That was doable. Right?

I brushed my hair and braided it back into a single French braid. That would keep it up and out of my face while we worked. And I had no doubt we'd be working today. After all, I'd been composing our to-do list half the night.

Downstairs, Sebastian was indeed making breakfast: waffles, eggs, bacon, hash browns, oatmeal, sausage, and French toast. Nero and Missy munched on their own plate of sausages quite happily. I stared at the scene, unable to speak at first.

"Holy crap, what are you doing? Shouldn't we be saving the food?" I managed to splutter the words out.

Sebastian flicked his head towards the hallway where the guest bedroom was. "She's going to be hungry. And let's be honest, this could be one of her last meals. Might as well make it a good one."

I swallowed my irritation. "You're a good man, my love, I hadn't thought of that." I caught him around the waist and lifted my face. He dropped a kiss on my lips and went back to the bacon sputtering on the stove.

I turned and walked to the guest bedroom door. Painted bright yellow, the color scheme wasn't something I'd gotten around to changing yet. The cheery colors seemed fitting for Jessica's personality and I was glad now I hadn't changed it. If these were her last few days as a human, the least we could do was help her be comfortable. I knocked three times. "Jessica, are you awake? We've got breakfast ready. Sebastian went all out."

A shuffle, and then a groan echoed through the door. I backed away thinking we'd made a serious mistake in letting her stay with us, even for the night. She'd already turned and now what did we do? How did we handle a Nevermore in our house?

The doorknob turned slowly and Jessica peeked out, with a big yawn as if she'd been up all night. "Is that bacon I smell?"

I let out a breath, relief rushing through me. "It sure is. Sebastian's been slaving over the stove all morning, just for you." I smiled at her and patted her back. She smiled.

"Of course, he did. He likes me." She flipped her hair as she passed me and headed into the kitchen.

I rolled my eyes. God save me from hormonal teenagers. She didn't know me at all, so she had no idea how little I was worried about the crush she had on my husband.

I followed her to the kitchen and sat as Sebastian put multiple platters of food on the table. I seriously doubted we'd be able to get through even half of it. Even with Missy peeking over the edge of the table in a most hopeful manner. I patted her on the head and she lay at my feet, placing herself between me and Jessica.

What happened next was like nothing I've seen before. Jessica, who couldn't have been more than five feet and weighed maybe one hundred pounds soaking wet, ate at least as much as Sebastian, who was a full foot plus taller than her and more than double her weight. To top it off, it looked as if they were in a race against one another. They popped sausages and bites of waffle into their mouths as fast as they could chew. The whole scene was more than a little disconcerting. I will admit it was rather funny to watch her face when she peeked under her eyelashes at Bastian. More than once she caught his eye and every time she did, he frowned at her. She'd stop with the flirting for a bit, focus on her food and then try again.

While they splurged, I had a single helping, keeping it to oatmeal and a banana. My stomach wasn't feeling well after all the excitement the day before and then lack of sleep.

"Oh, hell, why not?" I grabbed a few strips of bacon and chewed on them.

When the two of them finally slowed their rapid eating pace, I tapped a single knuckle on the table. "We've got a lot to do today."

"You got a plan?" Sebastian asked, looking from me to Jessica then back again.

"Of course." I gave him a wink. "I spent half the night thinking about things we could do. You've read a lot of Dan's books. Is there anything you can suggest before we run with my ideas?"

"All his stuff is about prepping before the world goes to shit. The thing is, I'm sure we can do some scavenging from other houses where people have turned into Nevermores, but I'm not sure how much we'll find."

I nodded. "Okay, I thought that we should make a tally of all the food in the house, plant the garden, and check fences today. I'd like to see about finding some information on the Internet while we can about stuff like candle making and food preservation. I mean, we can print it out and we've got it, no matter what happens."

"The fence is fine. I walked it last night," he said. "No holes, but we'll check it every day."

"What about the barbed wire?" I asked. We had the new square wire fence installed and hadn't even pulled down the old barbed wire on the other side.

He nodded slowly, chewing a mouthful. "A double fence I think is a good thing. It will help. I know the deer can jump it, but I don't think the Nevermores will be doing anything like that anytime soon."

I rubbed my face with both hands. "Well, as far as we know. What if there is some small hole you missed in the dark last night? At ground level where a Nevermore could crawl through. I'd feel better knowing you took a look today, just to make sure. They can't jump, maybe, but I bet they can crawl."

At that Sebastian paused, his mouth open to argue, then snapped it shut and nodded.

The thought of a horde of Nevermores pouring through a small hole was all too possible and all too frightening to take the chance that there was even one small opening on our first line of defense.

"We also need to find some way to store water." I leaned back in my chair, holding a piece of bacon in my mouth the way Dan held his cigar.

Sebastian nodded and leaned back in his chair, mimicking me, a curve of a smile on his mouth. "We can draw water from the well even when the power's out, but you're right, we should store some anyway. And I need to rig up a scoop or something so we can pull the water up once the power is done with." He stood. "I'm starting with the fences and throwing another chain and padlock on the front gate. Not like we're going to be using it anytime soon." He glanced at me and then Jessica. "Why don't you come with me, kid?"

I gave him a slight nod. Neither of us said what I was sure we were both thinking. The Nevermores saw her as one of their own and apparently they wouldn't hurt her, and that might keep Sebastian safer too, having her at his side.

Jessica nodded a little too eagerly as she took another bite of a sausage. Her face glowed with pleasure as she sucked the sausage into her mouth. Maybe it was just me, but Bastian looked like he paled some. Must have just been a trick of the light as the next minute his face flushed.

"You okay?" I reached over and touched his hand.

"Bit of spice is all," he muttered.

Jessica got up and ran back to her bedroom.

"Mara, that kid is trouble." He leaned toward me

and kept his voice down. "Serious trouble. Please be careful around her."

I frowned. "Why, because she has a crush on you?"

"Because she's close to turning."

My heart picked up speed along with my adrenaline. "Right."

"She could turn into one of them at any minute. We don't know how the process works. I'm going to keep her with me as much as possible. I'm big enough I can just sit on her if I need to."

So apparently, we hadn't been thinking the same thing.

"Well, it will keep her distracted hanging out with you." I punched him lightly on the arm. "And I understand if you have to sit on her."

She bounded out of her room with more than a spring in her step. "Ready to go."

He nodded at her and stood.

I grabbed Sebastian by the hand and pulled him back to me and planted a kiss on his lips. "Don't forget to reinforce the gate. I saw some extra bars in the grass beside it."

"Aye, aye, captain." He saluted me sharply and headed out, following Jessica's lithe figure.

After they left, I went straight to the computer. The news sites were on fire with videos and pictures I didn't need.

I sent emails to all my family members and as many of Sebastian's as I could. Just simple. We were okay, neither of us had taken the shot. Please let us know how you are. We love you. Be safe and God willing we will see you again. I broke down at the end, realizing that many, many of the people I loved the best were lost to Nevermore.

Lost.

I sobbed into my hands, and was brought out of it by Missy. She snuffled at my face buried on my lap.

"Thanks, honey," I whispered to her. Nero, puppy that he was, lay flat out on his back, sound asleep in a patch of sunshine.

Next, I tried to reach a few people by phone. No one answered and my heart clenched at the possibilities.

After that, I focussed on trying to get as much prepper information as I could printed out quickly.

Sheets and sheets on preserving food, making candles and soap, gardening, water collection, raising animals, butchering, medicinal herbs and how to use them, and of course, protection. I had a stack that was two inches thick by the time I was done, a veritable book on its own.

I stood and stretched and wandered back into the kitchen. The rest of the morning, I spent going through all our cupboards, charting out canned food and preserves, cleaners, toiletries, and perishables. Nero bounced around me trying to get me to play, but gave up after a short time,

Once I had everything stacked in order of how fast we needed to use it, my heart sank. I'd never really been a person to buy in bulk and it showed now in a most literal sense. There were three bags of pasta, less than two dozen cans of soup, one large bag of rice, eight cans of pasta sauce, seven cans of tuna, fourteen cans of fruit of various kinds, three boxes of Jell-O, one bag of flour and sugar each, a small bag of brown sugar, a half box of tea, one of each of my favorite spices, and that was about it for food of the non-perishable sort.

I scrubbed my hands over my face. The fridge was still full of fresh veggies and fruit, milk, cheese, half a dozen eggs, and two cuts of beef from dinner a couple of nights ago. The freezer was not so full, but there were a few bags of bread, ground beef, one package of bacon, a package of chicken drumsticks, and two frozen pizzas. How the hell were we going to make this stretch out for . . . what had Dan said? He was holing up until spring, which was easily eight months away.

"We are so screwed," I said softly, needing to break the depressing silence even if it was with a depressing statement out of my own mouth. Missy woofed in seeming agreement. I laughed and rubbed the top of her head.

I scrounged around in one of the cupboards and found a tennis ball. I rolled it across the floor, and the two labs bounded after it. Missy was so sweet and let Nero get the ball with minimal effort.

"You're a good mama," I said softly.

The normalcy of the moment was not lost on me and I kept playing with them to stretch it out as long as I could. But after only fifteen minutes of playing, Nero began to yawn. Missy butted him gently with her nose, knocking him over.

"Nap time, buddy." I scooped him up, grabbed a

towel, and once more made a makeshift bed in the tub. At least, there, he wouldn't get into trouble if he woke up and I didn't see right away.

Missy hopped into the tub with him and curled around her last remaining pup. Within minutes, they were both asleep. I left the bathroom door shut and wandered onto the back porch.

The sound of a huge rumbling engine reached my ears; a rumble that I recognized and had cursed most mornings as the neighbor and his god-awful diesel minus-a-muffler truck headed to work before the ass crack of dawn. Scrambling, I ran around the side of the house in time to see the horde in front of our gate scattered by the black Dodge. He mowed them down like a kid running through a field with a switch, carelessly cutting off the daisy heads.

Bodies flew out in all directions, screams of pain and rage coming from every quarter.

I shouted and pumped my fist in the air. Not because of the damage he was doing, but because his truck could get us out of here. It was big, it was bad, and it was ugly. Just what we needed to go . . . well, I didn't know that yet, but we could figure it out. The important thing was we could get out.

And that was all I cared about at the moment.

CHAPTER FIFTEEN

Sebastian

"Why did you want me to come with you? You change your mind about me now after you got a look at what I can offer?"

Jessica's words should not have surprised me, but to hear them out of her mouth when she was so young? It bothered me a great deal. In my mind, it was one thing for an adult woman to come onto a married man. But for a kid under sixteen? What had happened to her to bring her to this point?

"Stop feeling sorry for me," she snapped and I sucked in a sharp breath. This telepathy, or whatever it was between us, had to have an off switch.

"I want you to tell me how to block you."

"You don't want to know how I get in your head more?" she asked sweetly. I spun so quickly, she gasped as one hand wrapped around her throat. The pulse of her heart under my palm jumped and bucked but I didn't squeeze hard. I jerked my hand back, disbelief coursing through me. What the fuck was wrong with me? Violence was not my game; it was not my answer. Not ever. Not even in the worst hours of my life when . . . no. I was not letting my mind go back to that day.

Yet despite all that, strangling her to get an answer had been my first response. We locked eyes and she swallowed hard.

"It's the drug. It . . . brings out traits you kept buried . . .before." She rubbed at her neck, but the marks of my fingers had already faded. I arched an eyebrow, my anger still singing in my veins.

"You made a move on Dan before the shot?"

She shook her head. "No. A few days after."

She was lying. I was not going to let her think she could get away with that shit with me.

"Dan said it happened at a family dinner long before you got the shot." I stared her down and she lifted her chin.

"I barely touched his thigh then."

I hated to think there was some truth to what she was saying when I knew a portion of it was a lie. But I could actually see the differences in her now that she pointed it out. I'd met her before she'd gotten the shot and she'd been shy and sweet. None of this aggressive sexuality she displayed now. Understanding that wasn't really helping me cool my emotions.

"So you weren't always throwing yourself at men,

is that what you're trying to tell me?" I snapped the question at her.

Jessica flipped her hair over her shoulders. "I'm stronger now. I know what I want and I go after it instead of hiding behind my mother. I can help you control the mind reading . . .if you give me what I want." She pursed her lips. "You're going to be an alpha, I can feel it." She touched her fingertips over her belly and let them play down to the juncture of her thighs. I glared at her and took a few steps back, mostly to keep from striking out at her.

I just stared at her. "You're going to become a monster. That isn't stronger."

Her lips trembled and her eyes narrowed. "Are you sure about that? You were a pansy ass before, sitting behind your computer working. Already I can see your body changing. The same as mine."

My jaw ticked and I hated that she was right. Because I could feel my body changing, could feel the muscles flex and pull as though I'd been working out at the gym. And then there was my libido. If not for Mara, and my love for her, I'm not sure I would have walked away from Jessica's invitation. A very dark, very primal side of me urged me toward her. She was a fighter. A survivor.

An alpha like me.

No, we were nothing alike.

"I suggest you help me control wherever this anger is coming from, because right now the only person I want to hurt is you," I growled, and she shivered as though the sound had physically touched her. I twisted around and strode along the edge of the fence as I fought to get a hold of my anger.

The walking helped a little. The simple movement gave my boiling blood something to do. Somewhere to send the excessive energy that rolled through me. I hadn't slept a wink the night before, yet I didn't feel tired at all.

Jessica jogged to catch up to me and I snarled at her. Fucking snarled. She hopped a few feet to the side, putting distance between us. "I've decided to help you."

That surprised me, followed quickly by a deep suspicion. "Why?"

She shrugged. "To block another of the pack from reading your thoughts, you have to embrace the fact that you are alpha. It's that simple. If you aren't alpha, you don't have a choice of what the others see in your mind. But as alpha, you rule. No one can have your thoughts without permission."

I mulled over her words as I crouched by a stretch of fence that looked like it had been tested from the outside. I touched the black fur on the top strand of barbed wire on the inner, older fence. Bear, not Nevermore. "Not even you?"

"Maybe."

She wasn't being coy, I could hear the uncertainty in that single word. She didn't know a whole lot more than I did.

I pulled at the black fur and let it fall to the ground. The heavy scent of bear musk filled the air, cloying and. . . delicious. My stomach rolled and I clenched my jaw. I would not turn into one of the monsters. I refused to.

"Here, let's see if we can call some of the pack in. My dad and mom are in it, you know. My dad is the Beta. I think he's too old to be the Alpha or he would be." Jessica jogged ahead of me, her long blonde hair swinging back and forth. She looked like a child skipping through the field, switching off long stalks of grass as she went.

I followed her more slowly, still checking the fence for any breaks.

Jessica had climbed on a section of the fence that was braced with several pieces of wood, right at the corner. "I see them. But not my mom. I don't see my mom. Why isn't my mom with them?"

I put a hand on the tool belt slung from my waist and walked up beside her. I was tall enough I didn't need to sit on the fence to see what was going on. There were about fifteen Nevermores grouped together, some on the road, others sitting off to the side. The image was so strange because most still wore clothes, yet acted as animals. Business suits, skirts, jeans and even shoes in a couple of instances.

Jessica stared at them, her head going side to side. "Why isn't my mom here?"

I searched the pack with my eyes, not picking out the tell-tale blonde hair either. "I don't know. Could be another pack took her?"

As soon the words slipped from me I knew that wasn't the case. An image flickered through me, coming from the small Nevermore closest to me. He was the scout, the one sent out to find new food and shelter. And he'd seen Jessica's mom get shot by a human.

Jessica slumped, her hands barely catching her on the fence. I grabbed her around the waist and lifted her off. "I'm sorry."

"I thought . . .I thought we'd still be together."

I crouched beside her. "Your father is out there."

"He's . . . he can't protect me. He'll probably hurt me," she whispered. "It was always that way before. She tried to stop him. And now she isn't there." Tears trickled down her cheeks. Slowly, I grasped what she was saying.

"You don't mean he hit you, do you?"

She shook her head. "No. I wish he had."

I might regret it later, but I had a soft spot for the broken down. I'd spent most of my life looking after my mom and Gran, taking care of them after my dad and brother died. I put an arm around Jessica.

"I'll take care of you. When the time comes and I . . . when I turn. I'll take care of you. I won't let him hurt you ever again."

Her arms wrapped around me, every pretense of the hard and wanton young woman gone in a flood of tears and soft sobs. "Why?"

"Because I don't think you're really all that bad," I murmured into her hair. More than that, I couldn't leave her to her father. If he'd used her like that before he turned . . .how much worse would it be now with nothing but animal instinct driving him?

We sat for a few minutes and I waited until her tears subsided.

"Promise me you'll behave from now on. No more trying to seduce me. No more trying to tell Mara that . . . that I'm going to turn. I'll tell her, but for now—"

"I'll keep your secret." She tipped her head back and kissed me on the cheek and for a moment I saw the girl that I'd met at the mailbox. The tiny, shy girl with the beautiful smile and gentle voice.

She grabbed my upper thighs and squeezed hard, sliding them up fast to my package. "Because I know, as well as you, that the minute you're on that side of the fence, you're all mine."

I shoved her off me and she tumbled away, laughing.

God, I did not want to turn into a violent maniac. I could hurt Mara.

I left her there, laughing, and alternately sobbing. I felt bad for her and at the same time wanted to strangle some sense into her. I worked along the fence, finding two small spots I patched together with extra tension wire I had for fence repairs. I wove the strands back and forth more times than I would have normally. I had to make this place as safe for Mara as I could.

Because no matter how much I hated what Jessica said, she was right about one thing. There would come a time when I would need to be on the other side of the fence to keep my wife safe.

I pressed the heels of my hands into my eyes as I fought the urge to throw my head back and howl. No, it would do no good. I had to find a way to get Mara ready to do this on her own.

All of it. And she would need an escape plan, too. There was a good chance, at some point, she would either be forced to leave the farm, or she chose to in order to find other survivors she could work with.

My heart twanged with the thought of her moving on without me. Would I follow her? Or would I be bound to my new life here as a monster? My stomach heaved and I dropped to my knees as I lost most if not all of my breakfast.

I heaved hard, until my stomach ached and my throat was raw with bile. "Well, that was a damn waste of food." I wiped the back of my hand over my mouth, then spit to the side. I pushed to my feet.

I had to keep going. I had to be strong for Mara.

The rumble of a diesel engine snapped my head around and I stared as a flash of black shot down the road.

"Jessica!"

"I see it."

We bolted in tandem, and the strangest thing happened.

It was as if we synced with the pack, our bodies and hearts pulsing in time with theirs. A rush of strength shot through me and I moved as though I were one with the earth and air around me. As though every miniscule hump and dip in the earth was known to me and I avoided them with ease.

Joy, it was nothing short of amazing, this feeling.

As though I were flying, my legs and arms powering me through the world.

"Unreal," Jessica breathed.

I kept my mouth shut because the exact same word had echoed through my own mind.

But the feelings shattered as we rounded the side of the house, and the diesel engine mowed through the Nevermores and their pain became mine. I grunted as though I'd been hit and I stumbled, unable to keep the pace up. Jessica was no better as she sucked in a sharp breath and struggled to do more than that.

"We have to stop him," she whispered. "We can't let him hurt them."

"Wrong side of the fence," I said. But I wasn't sure if I meant her.

Or me.

CHAPTER SIXTEEN

Mara

My jubilation and thought that we had a way off the property was short lived. The big black Dodge lurched to a stop just past our house and I frowned at it as if my irritation would be enough to encourage it to go. Sebastian and Jessica ran in from the far field, tools in their hands, worry written across their faces.

"Mara?" Sebastian did a half turn, looking for me.

I stepped away from the side of the house so he could see me. "I'm here."

He hurried to my side and slid an arm around my waist. "What happened?"

"I don't know. I guess it just stalled out?"

The three of us stared as the truck engine rumbled for a second as though the driver was trying to get it going again. It coughed, and fell silent, choosing this moment to protest its rough usage over God only knew how many years. With the burnouts and horrid stench of black smoke that had greeted us every morning on the neighbor's way to work, I wasn't really surprised. The guy didn't even let the engine warm up. Just turned it on and hit the gas pedal.

The horde of Nevermores swarmed the truck, scratching and screaming at it. Their nails on the metal made my skin jump and twitch. Nails on metal was not something I would ever get used to.

"What's he doing?" Jessica leaned forward, taking half a step and then stopping herself.

"I think Mara is right and his truck stalled out. He might be able to get it going again," Sebastian said.

The back window of the truck slid open, and hands emerged. Our neighbour squeezed himself into the back of the truck bed.

"Hey!" he yelled, "Little help?" He flapped his arms and pointed around him like we hadn't noticed the Nevermores surrounding him, or like we had some magic wand that would carve a path for him through the horde.

"What are we supposed to do? Walk out there and ask them if they would mind not eating him?" I said, not really expecting an answer.

Jessica nodded. "They let me through once; they'll let me through with Tom. Or at least, they won't hurt me and I'm the best shot he's got. Right, Sebastian?"

He glared at her, and I put a hand on his arm, but it was her I spoke to. "Jessica, you don't know they won't attack you. As much as it's great you want to help him, you could both end up being killed."

"They didn't attack us on the back of your property when I was with Sebastian. They just stared at us. Besides. My dad is out there. He won't hurt me." Her voice wavered at the end and she glanced at Sebastian. "None of the males will hurt me. I'm sure of it."

Chills rippled over me at the sudden and vivid picture that rose in my mind. What Dr. Josephson had said on the TV slid into place right with what Jessica had just stated. My mind filled in the missing bits, and the understanding was nothing short of monstrous.

The horde worked like a wolf pack with an Alpha male and female, and the rest acting together as hunters and protectors. I sucked in a lungful of air at the horror of what I saw. The simplicity of the Nevermores making more sense than I would have thought. The pack, or whatever it was, wanted Jessica. If Dr. Josephson from the TV was right and the Nevermores were working like a wolf pack, they'd be looking for females to increase their numbers.

Oh. My. God.

More pieces of what was in front of us slipped into place. The drug made people more fertile, made them territorial, ravenous, and made them disease resistant. The population of Nevermores was going to boom at an incredible rate. They weren't zombies, they were a new breed of animal . . . one that would outstrip humans. And if the genetics didn't pass the drug to their young and make new Nevermores, I had no doubt what they would be eating for their next pack meal.

"No," I said, startling both Jessica and Sebastian. "You can't go out there. I won't let you." I moved to stand in her way. "They want you, the pack—horde, whatever it is, they want you." I swallowed hard. Sebastian stood behind Jessica, frowning.

"What are you talking about, Mara? She hasn't turned yet." But there was doubt in his voice. Like maybe he'd caught on to what I was talking about.

"Hey, come on, guys, don't leave me hanging here!" Tom yelled and the pack went wild with the sound of his voice. They were all but climbing on each other—at least as best they could—to get to him. He pressed himself against the cab of his truck, staying in the center.

"Keep your panties on, Tom!" I yelled back. I focused on Jessica again. "A breeder, that's all you'd be. Something to make babies and those babies will be just like them." I flung my arm out behind me. "And if they aren't, you can guess what's going to happen to the babies. They're going to be eaten. Just like Missy's other puppies were eaten."

Jessica paled and Sebastian frowned at me, flushing bright red all the way up to his hairline.

"They'd . . . you're right. They'd eat them," she whispered. I nodded.

"You don't know that, Mara," Sebastian snapped at me, "and you're scaring her."

"It's the truth," Jessica said. "I feel them pulling at me, wanting me to come to them. Especially that one there." She pointed to a big male who stood back from the rest of the pack, overseeing their efforts to pull Tom down who was now on the roof of his truck. The leader stood with his hands on his hips, and his eyes narrowed as he grunted and barked what seemed to be orders to the rest of the group. He was taller than the rest but not near as big as Sebastian. He had light blond hair that was twisted with mud on one side as though he'd been tousling with someone. I would guess he was in his mid-thirties, but it was hard to tell with the changes the drug had put him through. The male had a definite air of command around him though, and I had no doubt who was in charge of this pack. Trouble, that's what he was. To the side of the big male stood Jessica's father, the Beta of the pack. He had eyes for his daughter. And not in a way that I liked for one second. They were hungry, lusting eyes and even as I watched him looking at her, his flaccid dick began to stiffen.

Jessica, on the other hand, stared at the big blond male, completely ignoring her father. Her eyes didn't move from the Alpha for even a split second. And it wasn't a look of fear that washed over her face—but desire. Shit.

She pushed past me and headed straight toward the gate.

"He won't eat the babies; he'll keep them safe. I know he will. I'll come back after I get Tom out. I don't have to go with the pack yet." The certainty was strong in her voice as she climbed the gate and dropped lightly on the other side. The pack made room for her, touching her lightly, stroking her hair. She walked straight up to the big male, and brushed her fingertips against his. He stared down at her and she shook her head, and then pointed at Tom.

Sebastian shifted on his feet.

"Is she negotiating with him?" I whispered.

"How would I know?" he grumbled. He had a point.

Still, despite how the pack was treating her, I was not sure this was a good idea at all.

The big male shook his head, then roared. The pack scattered, leaving the truck clear.

"Tom! Hurry your ass up, man!" Sebastian yelled when Tom hesitated. Another breath and he jumped down from the truck and started to run toward our gate.

"Shit, I forgot my stash," he yelped and turned back to the truck. He grabbed the handle and I grabbed Sebastian's hand.

"Forget your weed, man! Move it!" Sebastian yelled.

"He's not going to make it," I whispered.

"He'll make it," Sebastian said.

One of the young male pack members crept forward, and sniffed the air, saliva rolling from his mouth in thick droplets. His hands clenched once, and his eyes rolled back in his head. A low keening rolled from its lips and finally it lunged at Tom, unable to control the ravenous desire.

I stifled a scream and Sebastian grabbed me, hugging me to him. But I couldn't look away. The scene had captured me too completely.

Tom yelled for us both, and the piercing cry rose in crescendo and pitch with each breath he took. Like the scream of pain unleashed the rest of them, the remainder of the pack rushed the two tousling figures, and Tom disappeared under a flurry of bodies, grasping hands, and slavering mouths.

Jessica snarled, and a few of the Nevermores slowed. She tried to run to Tom, but the big male reached out and snagged her around the chest. He held her tightly against his body until she stopped squirming, and her eyes glazing over with resignation. Or maybe desire, I wasn't entirely sure.

"Don't hurt him!" But it was too late and we all knew it. The pack didn't listen to her any more than they listened to Tom's pleas for mercy.

The strange hold that the unravelling scene had shown me let loose and I buried my head into Sebastian's chest.

"Look," Sebastian shook me gently, "It's done, but look."

I turned to see the pack retreating with their prize; none of it even recognizable as human any longer. Jessica and the Alpha male walked to the gate. He stood a few feet behind her and a low steady growl rumbled out of him. As if he were trying to stop her, but wasn't sure how to do it.

"Thank you. I wish I could have stayed with you longer," Jessica whispered as silver tears pooled in her quickly shifting eyes. She reached through, and though Sebastian grunted at me and made a move as if to bat my hands away, I took her hands and held them with my own. I rubbed my fingers over her knuckles and squeezed her hands tightly.

If she were my daughter, my child, I would want her to have this last moment. This one last connection with her humanity. I'd want her to be able to touch one of her own kind before she forgot everything she was and everything she could have been and turned into a monster.

"I wish we could've done more." I realized then how right Sebastian had been to take her with him to check the fences. I had no idea how close she'd been to turning. Bastian stepped up so he stood right behind me and slipped one hand around my waist. Across from us, the Alpha male growled and narrowed his strange eyes. Every muscle in the Nevermore's body tensed as though he was ready to leap over the fence and tackle Bastian. But instead, the Alpha's arms tightened around Jessica, tugging her back. I held onto her hands as tightly as I could but she began to slip.

"Jessica…" I wanted to say more than that. So much more.

She tipped her head and snarled at the Alpha, and amazingly, he eased off.

I pulled her hands up to mine and kissed the back of them. "I know . . . I know it isn't much. But be safe, Jessica. As safe as you can." I looked at her hands, really looked as I spoke.

The skin underneath my lips spun into a dusky yellow that was dissected with faint lines. The marks looked like veins, but weren't. They were images of yellow teardrops like a poorly drawn tattoo of a broom flower. The plant was taking hold of the humans it inhabited like it did the land it was introduced into. It encroached on everything it touched.

Jessica stared at us, no, stared at Sebastian. "You promised."

He nodded once. "I did. And I always keep my word."

The Alpha male pulled her away again, but not before giving Sebastian one more glare that bordered on hate. And maybe a little fear, which made no sense to me.

"I don't think he likes me," Bastian said.

"You think?" I turned away from the gate, my heart heavy with losing Jessica. Though I'd known it would happen, I just didn't think it would be so soon. I reached up, took Sebastian's hand off my shoulder and wrapped it around me, taking comfort in the warmth of his palm. If only I could so easily ward off the chill in my heart.

CHAPTER SEVENTEEN

Sebastian

Mara took Missy and Nero out in the back field to walk, but I knew that wasn't the only reason. Seeing Tom taken the way he was, and then losing Jessica had shaken her. Hell, it had shaken me . . . but I'd been seeing it from inside the other Nevermores' heads. The flickering images like a scattered movie screen as if the film jumped and skipped. I understood what was going on, but I couldn't hear the words clearly.

I rubbed my hands over my face and went into the house.

Jessica . . . just like that, she was gone and I wouldn't have to deal with her advances anymore. Then again, she had made a valid point. It would be five to six weeks based on what we knew, and I would be making my own trek over the fence to be with the Nevermores. To be a part of the pack.

My hand shook as I filled a large cup of water and guzzled it down. I refilled it and slumped into the chair in front of the computer. I clicked on the mouse and watched as the screen filled with images all over the world.

Over and over, it was the same thing as I slid through the images and headlines. So many people had taken the shot that there was no escaping the monsters. Most of the heads of state and government officials had taken the shot so the idea that someone was running the world was out the window. Same with most armies as they saw it as a way to keep their men and women healthy and fighting longer.

I clicked over to my email and checked the inbox. Normally it was full, messages from friends we'd left behind in the prairies, and new clients wanting work.

Nothing but a letter from Gran.

"You two kids take care of each other. I'm going to hunker down here and let it play out. Love you both. Don't be stupid."

It was signed simple. "Gran." No love and kisses. I smiled. That was my Gran all right. I wondered what she was up to in London, how she was faring against the Nevermores who growled with an English accent. She'd moved there from Canada only a few years before. She'd always wanted to live in the country of her origins and when she'd gotten the chance, she'd taken it. To her, life was a gift that you never walked away from. You wanted to live, then you did so with gusto.

What would she say to me now?

I picked the phone up and dialed through to her

flat before I changed my mind. What surprised me was that she picked up.

"Who is it?" She bit the words out and I smiled at the tone. I would not want to cross her.

"Gran, it's me, Bastian."

"Oh, Bastian! Are you two kids okay? You got my email? We aren't going to be able to reach each other soon you know."

"Mara is good. We're safe on the farm." I paused, wondering how to say what I needed to.

She beat me to it. "Bastian. Spit it out."

I drew in a breath. "I took the shot, Gran. Yesterday. Before . . . before they shut it down."

The silence on the other end made me wonder if we'd been cut off at first. "Gran?"

"My boy," she whispered and the break in her voice undid me. Tears slid down my cheeks.

"I thought . . . I thought it was the right choice. The fertility . . ."

"What does our Mara say?"

I didn't answer which I suppose was answer enough.

"You have to tell her, Bastian. You have to."

"What do I do, though? How do I help her?" I clenched the phone hard. "I mean, essentially it's a death sentence, one I can't change. She's going to be on her own and," I looked over my shoulder to make sure she wasn't sneaking up on me, "I'm going to be one of those . . . things."

Gran was quiet a moment. "I'll tell you what I think. I think you love her, more than you ever knew you could love. And if that isn't enough to fight off the instincts of these drug induced humans, I don't know what is. You trust your heart, Bastian. Don't let the drug take you, and you protect her. You take care of her and make sure she knows how much you love her. That's really all that matters in the end."

I closed my eyes. "I love you, Gran. You were . . . you were my mother, you know that."

She sighed. "Your momma didn't mean to turn away from you. You look so much like your father, she couldn't bear to look at you after he was gone."

I knew that, but even so . . . I had to make sure Gran knew. She was right. Love was all you had at the end. "But you ... you raised me, Gran. I love you, don't you ever doubt what you mean to me or Mara."

She sighed into the phone and there was a sharp boom on her side of the phone. She gasped and the phone went dead. I stared at the phone and then frantically tried to dial through to her. Nothing. The line was dead on her end, not even going to voice mail.

I put the phone down, slowly, as if that would somehow negate what had just happened. The back porch creaked and I stiffened in my chair until I recognized Mara's perfume.

"Holy shit," I whispered. I smelled her perfume from how far away, with walls between us? I stood and made my way through the house. It was only then that I realized the breeze coming through the kitchen window that looked out over the porch had brought her perfume into me. I started to laugh at myself. "Idiot, you think you're a damn superhero now or something?"

Mara stepped into the kitchen, the two dogs bouncing around her. She was a beauty, and I'd known it from the moment I'd met her. Her blue-gray eyes, the tilt of her lips, the soft flush of her cheeks and the way her hair curled down out of its pony tail as if escaping its bonds.

"You're my superhero, you know that?" She crossed the short distance between us and threw her arms around my neck. I bent and scooped her up, holding her tightly to me. The instant pulse of lust that rushed through me caught me off guard. I held her weight with one hand and lifted the other to the back of her head, so I could touch the silky soft strands that floated around her face. "I need you, Mara. More than ever."

Her lips parted and she kissed me hard enough that I was sure her lips would bruise. I clasped her to me, wanting nothing more than to rub my face over her, to mark her as mine.

Mark her.

I groaned and she thought it was eagerness. I let her go. "I need to . . ."

"Yes?" She nibbled at the edge of my shirt, working her way down to the top button.

"I should check the rest of the fence." I pushed her away as gently as I could, but I knew it would hurt her. I knew I was going to hurt her no matter what I did.

No matter how this ended, the ending was going to be the same. I would be gone, and Mara would be left to face this broken world on her own.

I stumbled along the opposite fence line, the one that was on the southern side and the one where . . . where Dan had said there was a trail. A woof spun me around and I watched as Missy bounded up to me.

She was a bit hesitant and I knew why. "I am starting to smell like them, aren't I?"

It would make sense, as much as I hated it. I crouched to her and held out a hand. "I'm doing my best, Missy. You've got to look after Mara when I'm gone. Okay?"

Her big brown eyes seemed to be full of understanding and she sniffed my hand once, then sneezed. I think she winked at me, but maybe I was seeing things. Maybe that was a part of being a Nevermore, too.

I snapped my fingers and she heeled to my side sticking to me, which was a bit of a surprise. We both knew what I was becoming. Yet, still, she trusted me.

We found the section Dan had talked about and the red ribbon marking it.

Dan could help her survive. I reached out and touched the ribbon, running it through my fingers. He could help her and I would convince him to. Somehow.

But once I talked him into it, would she listen to me and let the old codger teach her?

That I wasn't so sure about.

CHAPTER EIGHTEEN

Mara

The next week we spent digging the garden in, watering it daily, checking fences, and drinking lots of water to keep our hunger at bay in an attempt to food ration. Nero and Missy romped at our feet. Nero was oblivious to the danger around us, though he quickly learned to stay far away from the fence line. Only once did he stray close to the front gate. Missy had intersected him as a pair of hands reached through the slats for him.

She'd bit the hooked fingers and the Nevermore had reared back, screeching. Nero ran as fast as his stubby legs could carry him.

Very few of our family and friends responded to our emails, and even fewer to the phone calls we managed to get through.

We argued about whether or not to go to Dan's, but I won out. Or at least, I thought I did.

"Fine, Mara. Fine. We won't go to Dan, but I am going to see him," Sebastian said, his body slumped on the couch.

"We can't trust him, Sebastian. He came here to raid us, not help us, he said so himself. We're safe here. The Nevermores can't get in. If it comes down to desperation, then yes, maybe then we could go to Dan, but he's a last resort. He has to be," I said and went back to attempting to hand-stitch a patch on a shirt.

"You don't think this is a last resort?" he snapped, his anger shocking me. Fear was making him into a man I wasn't sure I knew.

I turned my face away from him, my jaw clenched tightly. I couldn't force him to listen to me. I knew that much. "At least . . ." I was going to tell him to wait. But the thing was, what would he be waiting for? Slowly, I realized he was right to want to strike out and see about reinforcing things—even if it meant involving Dan.

What I considered the "local pack" left us alone for the most part. The alpha (okay, I'm assuming here) sent out a scout once or twice a day. He was smaller than the rest, wiry and of indeterminate age. He was slightly hunched over with angry red slashes on his upper body and face, with a particularly bad one that went right across his forehead. The scout, who we simply started to call Scout, would rattle the massive gate by throwing his body against it, give us a growl, and then wander off.

The long hours, hard work, and emotional stress taxed us, made us both edgy and out of sorts, not even leaving us enough energy to make love, which was unusual for us.

Ten days in, which turned out to be the day before the power went out, we checked the TV as we did each morning and each night. For the first time in over a week there was an announcement and not just the looped video feeds we'd been seeing.

"Mara, come here, the TV's on," Sebastian called out. I ran downstairs, a towel wrapped around my hair. Water dripped off my legs and Nero licked it up off the floor.

On the TV, there was no announcer. Instead it was just a single picture like a page out of a book that scrolled up on a continual loop.

I read it out loud as it went. "All areas of North America are now considered uninhabitable territory as is the north and west of South America, all of Australia, Europe, and much of Asia."

There was a long stretch of blank screen and then a last warning.

I read it slowly, disbelief and a low thrum of resignation mixed with horror settling over me like a crushing weight of the ocean.

"All remaining residents from these named continents are now considered independent of any government, agency, or military command. We consider one area clear and free of the Nevermores. For those who are able, please make your way to—"

That's where it ended. The screen blinked and slid into white fuzzy static, reminding me of the twilight zone. I grabbed the remote and turned the TV off.

"What does that mean? They are giving up on us? On the antidote?" I asked, already suspecting the answer, but wanting Sebastian to say it out loud.

He reached up and took my hand. "We're on our own, babe. That's what it means. No one's going to come help us or try to get us out of here. They're going to let nature take its course, just like Dan said, and hope the Nevermores die off and the rest of humanity survives." He closed his eyes and a shudder rippled through him.

I squeezed his hand and slid into his lap. He circled his arms around me and we held each other, the fear surrounding us—right here was all we had left, the only place of safety in our world. "We've still got each other," I said.

Sebastian didn't answer me, just laid his head against my breast, his breathing uneven as if he were holding back tears.

He stood with me still in his arms. "I need you."

I kissed him hard, and he held me tightly as he walked to the bedroom. He kicked the door shut and laid me out on the bed. We made love and with it was an underlying sense of desperation, almost identical to the first day we'd seen the TV announcement. Bastian's body had hardened even in the last ten days, his muscles strengthening and his waist slimming at a rate I'd never seen on him. His stamina and energy had skyrocketed which led to only one thing. The session in the bedroom was . . .

"That was damn near a marathon," I breathed out.

I lay on my back, Sebastian's head on my belly. He laughed softly, but there was an edge to it.

"Are you complaining?"

I rubbed at my neck and the sudden onset of hives that crawled over my skin. "Ahh, no, but I need to get some medicine. I'm breaking out."

He jerked upright and stared at me, horror flickering through his eyes. "Your allergies?"

"Yeah, I guess." I reached for the side table where I kept my antihistamines. I popped two into my mouth and dry swallowed them.

"You're allergic to broom," he said softly.

I raised an eyebrow. "Um. Yeah."

"Shit." He spun, grabbed some clothes and left the room. What the hell was going on with him?

"Bastian?"

"I'm going to check the fences," he called back.

My shoulders slumped. I had no idea what was wrong with him, but when he was ready, he would tell me. That was his way. I knew it. Even if I thought it was stupid.

The next day, the power finally went and in the evening, we had to break out the flashlights and candles. We hoarded them, using them only when necessary. It was at that point that we realized we needed to dig a latrine of some sort because there would come a point where the septic tank would be full of, well shit. Shit—in the most literal sense of the word.

Worse than that realization was the fact that we were through half our food stores—not that we had much to begin with—and our garden was a long way from producing anything edible.

"We're just going to have to cut back more," I stared at our already meagre meal of pasta and a half can of tuna cooked over the barbecue. Sebastian had rigged the grill so we could cook with wood.

Come winter, we could use the wood stove in the living room, and the old wood-burning stove I'd thought to replace for heat would be perfect for cooking. But there were so many things on the list of needed items: candles, seeds for the garden, canning equipment, medical supplies, and basic pantry items like salt, sugar and flour, just to name a few things.

The two of us stood in the kitchen, the bare cupboards staring back at us. Sebastian scrubbed his hands through his hair, and his wedding band caught the last rays of the setting sun. I watched as it slid around, bumping up against his knuckle. The weight we had both lost was a testament to our hard work and lack of nutrition the last couple of weeks.

I started to laugh at the irony of the situation.

"What's so funny?"

I gulped the laughter down enough to answer him. "We've wanted to lose weight for so long, and all it took was for the world to shut down." Another peal of laughter ripped its way out of me, leaving me shaking and gasping for air, as tears ran down my cheeks. Hilarity rarely gripped me and now I seemed unable to shake its grasp as it roared through me.

He frowned at me, which only made me laugh harder; lack of food, poor sleep, feeling disconnected from him, and add on to that all the physical work we'd been doing made me giddy. I sat on the floor and the laughter rolled out of me. Nero dancing around my head woofing, which made me howl all the louder. Missy let out a low whine of concern, but I barely heard it.

Sebastian got up, left his plate of food and went outside. The back door slammed behind him, but I didn't care that he'd left, at least not in that moment.

I lay on the cool tile of the kitchen floor 'til the laughter subsided and the tears threatened to start. I forced them back, refusing to let them get a hold of me. I wouldn't let the fear rise again. We weren't going to die here. We were going to live and survive. Nero lay on one side of me and Missy on the other. "You two, you are too perfect to be believed." I put a hand on each of them. Nero was taking to his sit-stay commands so well, I wondered if someone had pre-programmed him for training. I couldn't have handled an unruly dog with all that had been happening. I let my hands rest on Nero's quickly-growing body, and Missy's still healing back. What were we going to do about them? We could barely feed ourselves and the dog food was diminishing as quickly as our own with the two of them eating the big bag down.

I stood slowly, wobbling a little. The distant thud of axe and wood told me where Sebastian was—not checking the fences then.

I ate half my meal and covered the rest with plastic wrap, something else we were nearly out of.

Crap. I knew I'd made a mess of it with Bastian,

and I needed to make things right. I headed outside, Nero and Missy at my heels. I balanced Sebastian's half eaten dinner in one hand.

He was at the back of the house, chopping wood with a serious focus that was a bit unnerving. Like he thought he was going to get through the entire pile in one session. Sweat dripped down his rapidly slimming frame. He would always be a big guy, but it was scary to see how fast he, especially, was losing weight with the restrictions on us.

"I'm sorry. I've pulled it together," I said in between chops. Sebastian lowered the blade and half turned to me.

"It's okay. I suppose from time to time you're going to have breakdowns. It's to be expected. As long as you can always pull yourself up and out of it," he said. I handed him his plate and he sat on a log to eat. His stomach rumbled loudly, but he ate slow. Savoring each bite.

I touched his shoulder, rubbing it gently. "Well, it's not like I'm going to be here by myself, right? You're not planning on doing a walkabout in the middle of the night, go for some sort of marathon run to see if you can outdistance the pack, are you?" I smiled at him and he gave me a half-hearted smile back.

"No, not planning on it. I don't want to leave you, babe."

I blinked hard and fear curled through me, wrapping itself around my throat. Was he trying to say something without saying it? Missy whined softly at my side, carefully putting herself between me and Sebastian. Cold chills rushed through my body.

"What's wrong, Bastian? I know this is a crap situation. I know it's not how we planned our lives, but we are alive and we still have each other. That's all that matters. We can do this. I know we can. Please don't give up hope." I sat beside him. A rattle drew our attention to the gate. Scout made his presence known as he body slammed the metal several times, more than usual for him. He grunted and pointed at the food on the plate in a rather frantic manner.

Sebastian stood and walked to the gate without a word. Missy gave a low bark and Nero whined in the back of his throat as Bastian drew closer to the Nevermore. Scout backed off a couple of feet, obviously intimidated by his size until Sebastian held the plate of food out to him.

"What are you doing?" The scene before me was . . .disturbing to say the least. Why was he showing kindness to the Nevermore? Why would he give him food that we had so little of, which we so desperately needed?

Scout slunk forward cautiously, his eyes downcast until he was right at the gate. Sebastian towered over him. One shaking, dusky yellow hand reached out to grab some noodles, streaking back to his mouth so quickly, I could barely track it with my eyes.

A second time he reached out to grab the food and as his hands grasped noodles, Sebastian's big hand clamped down on his arm. Scout squealed - which set Nero and Missy off. They barked in tandem, one high-pitched puppy and one pissed off mama dog. Scout tried to pull away but couldn't. Sebastian held on to him, not doing anything but keeping him from leaving. Scout squealed and screeched so loudly and high I found myself on my feet, heart pumping ready to run.

"Bastian, he's calling the others," I said, fear blooming once more. We'd been almost back to normal; I could almost forget the scene of Tom's death, of the pack surrounding our property, of Jessica going off with the Alpha. But this single moment was bringing it all back in a rather unpleasant rush.

"I know," Bastian said.

Two words, so simple, and yet they meant so much. He wanted Scout to call the pack in, but why? It didn't make sense.

Rustling in the bushes was the only warning we had before the Nevermores exploded onto the road, screaming and gnashing their teeth. They were thinner than the last time I'd seen them, but they didn't seem worse for wear, otherwise, and it was obvious their energy was still high.

I searched the group, standing on my tiptoes and then finally climbing onto the chopping block in order to see. Was Jessica still with them? Had she survived the last couple of weeks?

"She's at the back!" I said. She was thinner than before, and her clothes were ragged, but unlike some of the others who had scars and missing pieces of hair, she looked . . . like the queen of the pack. Even her hair was cleaner and neater than the others.

The Alpha male with the blond hair stepped out of the bush and put his hand on her shoulder, claiming her while he stared at Sebastian. Her father stood to the other side of her and she cringed slightly from him, pressing into the Alpha.

"What does he think? That you're going to fight him for her?" I asked more to myself, but Sebastian heard me.

"That's exactly what he thinks. I'm bigger, stronger, and younger. A threat to his position in the hierarchy of the pack," he said.

"But you aren't part of the pack, Bastian. You're human."

Sebastian turned to look at me, his eyes sad, and his face etched as though he was pained.

My heart dropped, the world slowed, sound disappeared except for the hammering of my heart.

"Mara, the results from the fertility tests came back while you were out of it. It wasn't you who had fertility problems, it was me. The day I gave you Nero, that morning when I was in town . . .I talked them into letting me have the last shot." He barked a pained laugh. "I convinced them to let me have it, begged them. They weren't supposed to."

I shook my head and backed away, half falling off the chopping block and stumbling over Nero. "No, no you didn't. You wouldn't have. You said it was stupid, that there was no way you would ever . . ." The world swayed around me and I fell to my knees, grabbing at the axe handle for support as I struggled to breathe.

This was not happening. This . . . this wasn't real. A nightmare, I had to still be asleep.

Sebastian crouched beside me and turned my body so we both faced the gate and the pack beyond it. His hands were hot on my bare flesh and I began to itch . . . understanding rocked through me. "When we made love, and I got hives after—"

He swallowed hard. "The broom is in me and my sweat. You are allergic to what I am now. I didn't realize until . . . until the last time."

It made a horrible, awful sense.

I let out a moan and he held me tightly, his lips buried in my hair. He rocked me gently as I cried.

"I'm so sorry, Mara, that I took the shot." He looked me in the eye. His normally blue eyes had already begun to tint a light yellow. A faded dusky yellow that I'd been telling myself was just the way the light reflected on his iris at certain times.

"You took Nevermore?" I had to hear him say it out loud. To say the words to believe that this was happening.

He nodded, the left side of his jaw ticking. "I took Nevermore."

CHAPTER NINETEEN

Sebastian

They called to me from the other side of the gate, whispering in the way that they did that I was needed. That they were being hurt and it was up to me to protect them. That they wanted me as their Alpha. The pull wasn't overwhelming, but I knew there would come a point where it would be. I held Mara. Behind her, Missy locked eyes with me and slowly, she bared her teeth. Not a sound, but the warning was clear as her lips rippled back.

Missy would stand between us. She'd known all along what was happening to me and she'd always been subtle in her stance. Putting herself between Mara and me, or between Nero and me. Protecting her own pack.

Soon enough . . . I would have to go. I bit back on

the cry that wanted to escape my lips. Mara needed me to be strong for as long as I could.

An image so wild and unreal coursed over me.

Running through the woods, the smell of new growth, dying logs, and an animal running ahead of me, the scent of blood as the pack moved in from all sides, taking the deer down in a rush of hunger and excitement. The only thing that kept me grounded was Mara, holding to me as hard as I held to her.

I couldn't imagine losing my love for her, losing her as my mind disappeared. But maybe . . . maybe it wouldn't be so bad. I wouldn't know that I was lost. I would just be existing.

Without the love of my life, my other half.

What the hell was I going to do?

Chapter Twenty

Mara

I sobbed into his chest, pounded on it in a fit of rage. "How could you do this to me? You're going to leave me and forget me!" It was easy to forget that if I'd had my way, our situations would have been reversed. That even now I'd be with Jessica on the other side of the fence, trying to get in and kill Sebastian.

He said nothing, just held me as I flailed and beat at him.

Distantly, I knew that the pack dispersed. Once more they were stymied by the gate and their inability to climb or unlock it. With my head on Sebastian's shoulder, I watched them melt into the bush as if they had never been there.

All except Scout, who stared at us with his slitted eyes and rattled the gate to get our attention once more. I did the calculation in my head of the timeline since Sebastian had taken the shot.

My heart hiccupped. In less than three weeks, the place Scout stood could be where Sebastian would stand. Outside the property, an animal who no longer loved me, an animal who would as soon eat me as make love to me.

I stood, and pushing away from him, anger and pain at war with one another inside my heart. "I need to be alone."

He stared at me and a hardness filled his eyes. "You're going to get a lot of that in the not too distant future, probably more than you want. I would take advantage of the time we have together."

I spun on my heel, ready to slap him for the insensitivity. "You asshole! Why didn't you tell me you'd taken the shot the second you realized you were going to turn?"

He frowned and shook his head, "I didn't want you to worry. I didn't want you to stress more than you already were!"

That was horseshit. "It's my right to worry! I'm your wife, if anyone should know that you're going to turn into an animal, it's me!" I yelled at him, Nero whimpered at my feet, upset by the yelling. I bent and scooped him into my arms. Missy, on the other hand, had her hackles up and stood a foot in front of me, between Sebastian and me. The intent was clear. Keeping us apart. I didn't blame her.

He put his hands on his hips. "The right time didn't come up. And I wasn't sure at first, I didn't feel any different, and the dose was smaller. Like three quarters what it was supposed to be so I figured it might not have the full effect." The way he lowered his eyes, though, told me all I needed. He'd known. From the first, he'd known what was happening.

His behavior, the way he reacted to the TV announcements, the desire to get as much done as quickly as he could despite the toll it took . . . I saw it all in the way he wouldn't look at me.

He'd known.

I stomped toward the backyard and the garden beyond, the sudden urge to kill something leaving me only one option. Pulling weeds. Over my shoulder, I yelled, "You know, the right time was the minute you figured it out, jerk face."

I thought things couldn't get much worse.

Missy shot out in front of me as we rounded the side of the house. Barking, she scattered the three deer that stood in my garden. They had neatly pruned off every last shoot of vegetable that had come up in the last week. Apparently their ability to jump the fence gave them the edge over the Nevermores who also wanted in.

I wanted to cry. I wanted to yell and scream and throw things. I put Nero down, and as I did I scooped up a rock, and hurled it at the four-legged interlopers as Missy sent them running. I missed by an easy mile and had to settle for running at them full speed down a slight slope. Nero woofed and ran too but he wasn't any faster than me. The three of us followed the deer well into the open field. As they scattered and hopped the fence to avoid us, I slipped. I tumbled to the ground, my legs sprawled out under me.

I covered my eyes and sobbed. Anger and fear, hurt and grief like I'd never known filled me and spilled out my eyes and mouth.

Missy let out a low growl. I slipped an arm around her neck and hugged her tightly. "He's still okay, Missy."

"Mara." He spoke softly, carefully. "You're right. I should have told you. I was doing . . . what I thought was right."

He sat beside me and I tucked my face into the crook of his neck, breathing in his scent, trying hard not to think about what was coming. I had no words, though, I didn't know what to say because nothing could make this better. Nothing could stop what was going to happen to him.

And to me.

"I'll help you get ready, babe. I won't leave you here without the things you're going to need," he whispered into my hair.

"That gives me little solace when I know you won't love me anymore. Alone is one thing, but to have you close, and yet so far from yourself . . ." I whispered back.

He was silent for so long that I wasn't sure he heard me. It was the shuddering that started deep in his body that made me sit back. Tears streamed down his face, washing lines of dirt and grime away, leaving streaks of almost-clean skin.

"I will always love you, no matter how far my

mind goes, no matter what I become; my love for you will never change. I couldn't imagine my life with anyone else, Mara, and these last four years have been the best part of my whole life. I wouldn't change a thing." At my raised eyebrow he conceded with a half-smile, "Well, maybe one thing."

He stroked my face with his hands and he whispered against my lips, "I didn't tell you enough how much I love you. I didn't always cherish you the way I should have, but I will always, always love you, no matter what comes. No matter how ugly things get." He kissed me softly and I leaned into his mouth. If this was all I had left with him. I would take every minute of it; my anger washed away in a wave of love so strong, I thought my heart might burst with it. We clung to each other until the tide of emotion that swelled around us receded and we could both breathe a little easier. I leaned back from him to stare into the face that I would love no matter what it looked like. No matter what kind of monster he became, I would love him.

"What are we waiting for then? I took my antihistamines this morning," I asked, pulling him to his feet.

He cocked his head and stared at me. I winked and started to slide my shirt over my head. It took him a brief moment, then he was there helping me undress—and as I helped him—we made love in the garden. It wasn't like we were going to be damaging the crops or anything, and we took our time, savoring each touch, each kiss, as if they were our last, breaking only when Missy decided we'd taken enough time, and jammed her cold nose between us.

Her eyes said it all. She didn't trust Sebastian.

But she was wrong. I had to believe it. I would trust Sebastian.

No matter what happened.

CHAPTER TWENTY - ONE

Sebastian

Two weeks whipped by with the speed I usually reserved for knowing a prostate exam was coming and wondering if I could get out of it, but before I could, the day was upon me.

Mara had taken the news that I was going to turn into a monster better than I'd thought. Missy had continued to make sure I knew her stance on things. I only hoped the dog lived a long time and continued to protect Mara from everything as well as from me.

I'd managed to rig up a hand pump for the well, chop all the firewood that Mara would need for at least two winters, dig several latrines, and fortify sections of the fence I thought might be shoddy. We'd discovered a wild plum tree that hung over the back fence and had set to picking the fruit, stuffing them into the few jars we had on hand and made an attempt at canning them. There were patches where blackberries crawled through the field, red berries hanging heavy on them. I watered them daily, helping them along. At least they would give her some food after I was gone. The needs of the dogs were a bit harder, but they gamely ate whatever leftovers we gave them.

Through it all, my body burned calories and energy like nothing I'd ever experienced.

My physical hunger was eclipsed only by the desire I had for Mara's body. Sex had always been good between us, but nothing like the raging lovemaking that now went on daily. Sometimes twice a day. I literally couldn't get enough of her.

I wasn't sure if it was the drug, or my fear that I would be leaving her soon.

Maybe both.

Then the day came that I knew I could do nothing more for the farm. I just finished making the fence around the garden higher. Time to make my first foray off the property and find everything I could that Mara might need. She wasn't going to like it.

The sound of the gate rattling tipped my head in that direction. Scout again. I knew not because it was always him but because the images he gave to me were always the same. The plate of food I'd offered to him.

I made my way around the house. I passed the kitchen window, glanced in and saw Mara reading through her stack of papers she'd printed out the first day we'd realized what was happening. More than once we'd referred to the information in those papers, using them to help figure out the best placement of a latrine. How to can fruit. Mara had even made an attempt at making soap, though it hadn't turned out well, at all, and had been just a lump of fat that smelled lightly of lavender.

Scout grunted as I came into view. The images twisted into words inside my head more than ever before.

You come. Help us. Protect us.

I shook my head. "Not yet."

Father hurts girl. Alpha doesn't see. Too busy. Scout snorted and shook his head. I crouched by the gate, thinking. He had to mean Jessica.

Damn it.

No. She would have to wait. As much as I wanted to help her, save her from her father, the reality was Mara would always come first. Jessica second.

"Soon." I reached through and put a hand on the top of Scout's head. He flinched and then relaxed and slipped away.

Soon good. Now better. The thoughts were simple, but clearly intelligent. Whatever I was becoming there was at least that. I would have thoughts. I would have language. I would have someone to protect. I had to work to swallow the emotion that spilled up.

I cleared my throat and stood. My body froze, though, as I realized I was being watched.

Jessica stood across the road from me. Her young body was barely clothed, and her top hung halfway off her body showing off one breast.

The surge of lust in my body was all animalistic and nothing like me. I backed away, breathing hard.

She smiled and put a hand to her hip. A low keening moan slipped from her and I scrambled backward faster.

You want me. I want you. Take me. Make me yours. Mate.

I couldn't scrub the images from my mind so I ran until I was far enough away that I couldn't feel her in my head. Couldn't sense her at all.

Mara found me in the field on my knees.

"Bastian," she was out of breath when she reached me. "I saw you running are you okay? What happened?"

I grabbed her and rolled her under me, my mouth on hers in a flash of need stronger than ever before. She gasped but didn't pull back. I ripped her clothes from her, unable to slow down. Unable to take my time.

Mara was the love of my life. She was the one I wanted.

The only way I could think to drive Jessica out of my head was to hold onto my Mara.

We rocked together, climaxing fast and hard, multiple times. Out of breath, I rested on my forearms and pressed my forehead to hers. "I love you, babe."

"I love you, too," her lips were swollen. I hoped from my kisses but no doubt from her growing reaction to me. Though to be fair, it was only her lips this time. Perhaps she was growing accustomed to the allergens in my skin.

She smiled up at me, her skin glowing softly with a sheen of sweat. I kissed her again, and dared a lick along her cheek. The salty moisture seemed to invigorate me again and I shifted my hips against hers as I grew hard again.

Mara's laugh turned into a moan as she arched against me. "Don't let me stop you."

We went slower that time, taking our time. Holding each other as I stared into her eyes, knowing that I was far closer to turning than I wanted to admit.

Time. I needed time.

If only love was enough to give us that.

But even I wasn't that much of a fool.

Chapter
Twenty - Two

Mara

"I'm going, Mara. I have less than a week, a few days maybe, and it's a window of opportunity we can't let pass." Sebastian dressed quickly, pulling on jeans and a dark T-shirt that hung off him. It was early, pre-dawn, and we'd been arguing about this subject most of the night.

"Bastian, if the Alpha male catches you outside the gate, he'll attack you—we both know that. Maybe he'll even be able to turn the whole pack against you. As strong as you've become you won't survive an attack from the entire group." I shadowed my husband as he searched our closet for the extra knapsack.

"That's why I'm going so early. You know Scout's never been here before the sun is up. My plan is to raid as many of the houses as I can in the areas closest to us. You need the food and you can't go out. It's like with Jessica--they won't touch me. I'm one of them."

I snorted. "Nobody wants to get laid by you. That's what they wanted from her, and you know that."

He was quiet a moment too long. I touched him on the arm. "Tell me."

"Jessica wants me to become the Alpha, too. Her . . . interest in me started when she was here. Nothing happened."

"I never would have thought it did," I said softly.

He gave me a weak grin. "Besides, I can think of at least one person who wants to get laid by me that I'd like to oblige." He bent and kissed me on the lips, the tingle not all due to our chemistry. Mostly, now, it was due to the drug I was so allergic to rushing through his system. But the added sensations were not unwelcome, even I could admit that.

I followed him downstairs where he grabbed a flashlight, a hammer, and the big kitchen knife. In the dim light, he looked like a burglar, which was appropriate considering what he was going to do.

"Did you write me a list, at least? I don't want any complaints that you didn't get everything you wanted." He smiled at me, trying to ease the tension, I suppose. I let out a breath. He was going to do this whether I wanted him to or not. I had lost the battle in large part because I knew he was right. I needed him to get food and supplies, and he needed to do this one last thing for me, to be my husband and knight in shining armor. But I was terrified he would go . . . and never come back. Not because he had been hurt, or killed, though, that was a possibility. No, the deepest fear was he would turn into a Nevermore while he was out there and truly be gone.

I sat and lit a candle so I could see enough to write. The list was simple, any preserves he could carry, batteries, feminine hygiene products, any allergy medicine he came across—any medicine for that matter—a bow and arrow set would be awesome, garden seeds ... I tapped the pencil against my teeth. What else was there?

I shrugged. "I can't think of anything else. Anything that looks useful, anything we can eat or preserve. Any weapons you can carry, I guess."

Sebastian took the list from me and tucked it into his back pocket. "I don't know how long I'll be, babe, but try not to worry." He bent and kissed me good-bye, lingering for a moment. Our breath mingled, softened, and I tightened my hold on him.

"Come back to me," I whispered against his lips.

"Always, I'll always come back to you." He kissed me again, harder this time, and I knew if I didn't let him go now, I never would.

"Go." I pushed him away and kept my butt in the chair.

He rubbed a hand over his head once, leaned forward and blew out the candle. My eyes fought to adjust quickly to the semi-dark so all I saw of him leaving was the outline of his body, his broad shoulders and now narrow hips.

The door clicked closed behind him, and a sense of finality settled over me.

This was it, in little more than a week, I would truly be on my own. This was like a test run on what was about to be the rest of my life, however long it turned out to be.

I sat there 'til the sun rose, and warmed the room. The light of day forced me to admit I was on my own. Missy put a paw on my leg, whined and licked her chops.

"You got it. Breakfast coming up."

I fed the dogs, and myself our meagre meals. I had a bit of rice I'd made the night before and tossed it with a bit of sugar and cinnamon. Palatable for sure, but not exactly filling.

"I've got to keep busy," I said to the dogs who cocked their heads to the side in tandem. I laughed. "Come on, let's see what the day has to offer."

Not much as it turned out.

I cleaned the house, sweeping out the tumble weeds of dog hair and dusting what I could. Next was weed pulling and watering for the now defunct garden simply because I hoped that something might yet come up if I kept at it. The three of us walked the fences, checking for any damage. Lunch break. Pulled water from the well and washed clothes by hand, then hung them out to dry on a makeshift clothesline Bastian had made.

By late afternoon, I had done a lot, yet felt like I was spinning my wheels. The wood pile caught my eye. We had plenty of wood for the next couple of years, but Sebastian was right. I was going to have to learn to do this on my own. All of it.

Never having chopped wood in my entire life left me wondering if there was a technique or a method to the process. I scratched my head a moment, then pulled out a fir log that needed to be split, standing it up on end as I'd seen Sebastian do. Before my first swing, I pulled out the tennis ball I kept in my pocket and threw it into the field for Nero. He and Missy blasted off after it and I had my chance to swing without fear of hitting either dog. A distinct possibility that scared the daylights out of me.

I held the very end of the axe handle and gripped it like I would a baseball bat, then with one swing I brought it down, missing the log entirely and burying it into the dirt at my feet.

"Well, that's no good," I grumbled.

Rough laughter in the air shocked me, and I spun to see Scout watching me. He sat at the gate, crouched low and grinning in my direction. The dirty little bastard was laughing at my attempt to split wood? I'd like to see him try considering he had no fine motor skills.

I flipped him off and he laughed again and flapped his hands at me, as if egging me on.

To see glimpses of a human personality inside what I viewed now as a large, predatory animal was strange to say the least. They weren't zombies, they were most definitely alive, and they were far from mindless. From everything I'd observed, they really did act like a pack of wolves, hunting their food and sharing it amongst the group. I'd even seen them eating shrubs and berries, though it didn't seem to satisfy them any more than eating large amounts of meat. An image of

Tom being torn apart made me sway and I put a hand on the log to balance myself.

Yeah, maybe best not to think about someone being torn apart limb from limb in front of me.

Missy and Nero bounded up to the lawn behind me. Missy held the ball high, and Nero leapt for it, growling his little puppy growl. Like he was some big tough dog.

With the two of them still busy I picked up the axe again. I hefted it once more and swung hard. I managed to give the log a glancing blow. That'll teach it. Yeah, right.

I took a deep breath, stared at the log right where I wanted to hit it, lifted the blade for a third time and brought the axe down hard. The blade bit the center of the fir, and divided it cleanly in half. I dropped the axe in surprise and then did a dance around the two pieces.

Again laughter reached my ears, but I ignored Scout. This was a great moment, one I could be proud of. With no one to share with though made it more than a little bittersweet.

Now that I knew the trick, I chopped a few more pieces gaining proficiency with each blow, until my hands began to hurt and blister. Then I stacked the wood in with the rest. Sebastian would be proud.

After washing up out of a bucket of water I'd pulled from the well earlier, I went inside as the summer sun began to set.

"Come on, you two, time to eat!" I called over my shoulder. Missy and Nero bounded along, happy as could be. Only once did I see Missy look over her shoulder and stare at Scout. But no growl escaped her. She was getting used to his constant presence, too.

I wasn't sure that was a good thing.

Back in the house, I caught a glimpse of myself in the hallway mirror. I paused and really looked at my reflection. A few short weeks ago, my life had been about sleeping in, eating what I wanted, watching TV, and finding a way to get pregnant and now . . . .

I looked like a . . . I didn't even know what I looked like—not myself, that was for sure. My skin was deeply tanned, something I'd avoided the last few years working inside as much as I did. My hair had lightened with my natural dark brunette lightening with a good dose of red highlights. I turned sideways and ran a hand over my waist. It looked as if I'd lost fifteen or twenty pounds too. My clothes hung off my frame, something I hadn't noticed with all the chaos. Even my face had slimmed, with my cheekbones becoming more prominent, and the shape of my face more defined.

I shook my head, what did it matter now? It wasn't like we were going to have children or go on vacation somewhere warm where I could show off my body in a two-piece. There would be no prize for being thinner now.

Dinner consisted of three large glasses of water, two slices of what was my shitty attempt at making bread, and a can of tuna that I shared with the two dogs. There were a few plums on the counter which I also ate, knowing they wouldn't last. Nothing would and I was still learning how to preserve things. I sighed, pitted a couple of plums and gave them to the dogs. Missy ate hers happily, but Nero turned his nose up. The only good thing was that he seemed to still be nursing a bit from her.

Going up to our bed without Sebastian felt all sorts of wrong. Full as I was going to get, I headed to the living room, pausing at the butcher block. I slid the only other big knife we had from its holder.

"Just in case."

Missy seemed to nod in approval.

I fell asleep on the couch with the knife tucked into the cushion beside me, Nero curled up in my arms and Missy snuggled in tightly behind my knees.

Exhaustion rolled over me, sucking me down into its blissful depths, the only place I could escape to now.

I dreamed about Sebastian. We were on our long-awaited honeymoon, something we'd been planning to do for so long. There was a beautiful blue ocean, clear to the bottom so we could see fish and coral clearly as if it were glass and not water. Maybe the Caribbean or somewhere in Hawaii—I didn't know and didn't care. I only knew two things. We were together, and he wasn't a monster. He hadn't taken the Nevermore shot. We laughed and smiled about how we'd escaped the farm.

His skin was tanned and healthy, not a single yellow tinge on him.

I looked down at myself. Hell, yeah, I wore a two-piece bikini with a white gauzy sarong around my now-slim hips. The kind I'd seen super models wear on a beach shoot. I looked up with a smile on my lips. Sebastian was gone.

"Bastian?" My voice was eaten up by the waves and the sound of the crashing surf that rose around me.

"I'm here, babe." He was behind me, surprising me. His arms circled around my waist and I leaned into him with a sigh of relief.

"I thought you were gone."

He kissed my temple and let go of me, I spun in the wet sand, stumbling. In that split second he was already down the beach, walking slowly, bending every now and then to pick up something from the sand. I laughed and ran towards him, sprinting to cover the short distance between us. But no matter how hard I ran, no matter that he was only walking and I was running for all I was worth . . .I couldn't catch him. Farther and farther until he began to fade.

"Sebastian, wait for me!"

He didn't turn back, just kept on walking as if he couldn't hear me, his broad back disappearing into the distance.

"Sebastian!" I gasped his name as I threw myself out of the dream and off the couch. I hit the wooden floorboards hard. Nero rolled out of my arms with a grunt, his big eyes blinking up at me like "what the hell, I was sleeping?"

Missy let out a long, low rumbling growl. Breathing hard, I reached up and touched her. "It's okay, Missy. It was just a dream."

But she didn't calm, not for an instant. She stared at the door, her ears pinned to her head.

And footsteps pattered on the porch, the sound of multiple feet running.

Shit, shit, shit. I gulped down a breath and slid to the window, peeking up over the sill.

There were four of them and one of me. This was not good, not good at all.

CHAPTER
TWENTY - THREE

Sebastian

Leaving Mara behind was harder than even I'd thought. The minute my feet were on the grass behind the house, I ran for the back fence because I knew if I went any slower, I might not leave at all.

I'd set up a couple of logs on our side of the fence to help someone to get over easier. I leapt when I got close, hitting the first log and then using my momentum to clear the fence. To clear a five-and-a-half-foot fence.

I landed in the soft dirt on the other side in a crouch and looked over my shoulder. The house was awash in the soft glow of the sun as it peeked over the eastern trees. I shook my head and turned my back on it. With a quick adjustment of my pack, I stood and took a step, only to freeze where I was.

An image of a plate of noodles washed through my

mind. I spun and grabbed Scout around the throat. He went limp, his eyes wide and terrified.

He held up his hands in the universal sign of surrender. I dropped him and he nodded at the house.

You leave your mate?

I blinked. "Have to."

Want Scout to watch over her?

A chill swept through me. Would he? I guess it couldn't hurt, it wasn't like she was going to go outside the fence. "Yes, watch over her. Don't hurt her." I let an image of me strangling him, with Mara's body on the ground between us. Pretty much the best threat I could come up with on the spot.

He gave me a wink, grinned, then spun and disappeared around the side of the property. Headed for the gate.

I shook my head. "Shit."

I was conversing with animals. A regular Dr. Doolittle now. I snorted and settled into a ground-eating jog. My first stop was Dan's place. I made it to his bunker house in no time, and with nothing more than the odd rustle of bush around me. No Nevermores, no images floating through my head.

I'd worked on blocking the images, and I could if I was paying attention, but the thing was. . .it gave me an edge if I was open to them. More than once I'd 'seen' Nevermores in my head long before I came to a section of the fence I was checking where they hid. The distance seemed to range, but I'd figured I had at least a thirty-foot radius when I was concentrating.

It had been sloppy of me to let Scout creep on me the way he had.

Dan's house reared above me, silent in the early morning light. Around the side of the house was a pile of fish that were stinking to high heaven. What the hell was he up to?

Was he trying to draw the Nevermores to him?

"Shit, you are, aren't you?" That was exactly what he was doing. I crept forward, the smell of fish as rotten as it was pulled me forward. Saliva burst in my mouth until it dripped past my clamped lips.

I pushed the fish closest to me with a toe and it fell apart. Jaw clenched, I moved around the side of the bush trap. Some of the fish had a strange green slime on them. Poison? My nose twitched and I backed away. Dan had been . . . busy to say the least.

A low grunt, and a waft of bear rolled over me. I spun, but Bob was on the other side of the yard. He trundled my way, seemingly not bothered by my presence. Or so I thought.

He jerked to a stop and lifted his nose, sniffing the air. A barking cough erupted out of his muzzle, flapping his lips and showing his teeth.

The one door of the house creaked open and Dan stepped out with his gun raised.

"Bob thinks you smell like those Nevermores."

I held up my hands, thinking of Scout. "I ran into one on my way here. Had a tousle with him."

"You survived?" Dan's disbelief was heavy in the words.

"He was small. I'm not."

The three way stand-off held for another ten seconds before Bob broke it. He put his head down and charged me, roaring. I bolted for the house, and Dan stepped aside, letting me in.

I stumbled down the single step to my knees, spun and was up on my feet before Dan had shut the door.

"How do you keep Bob from eating the poisoned fish?"

Dan grunted and faced me. "He ain't stupid. Unfortunate for me, neither is that local pack. Jessica's part of them now, you see that?"

I nodded. "Yeah, we . . . she was with us right before she went over."

His eyebrows shot up. "And you didn't kill her?"

I glared at him. "She was still human."

"No, she wasn't," he growled. "The thing is, no one who took that godforsaken shot is human anymore and have to be treated like the animals they are. You kill them when you get the chance before they kill you."

He pushed past me. "I promised you a weapon. You want a rifle?"

I clenched my hands to keep from slamming a fist in to the wall, the aggression flowing through me truly a struggle to keep a hold of. "That's the most useful? For hunting and protection?"

"Yup. I'll even give you some ammo." He scrounged around in a box and pulled out two packages of cartridges. "Here. I'll give you my thirty aught six."

I didn't ask him what that meant. I didn't want him to think I was that much of a—

"You know how to use a gun?" He shoved a long handled rifle at me. I gripped the wooden butt and awkwardly stuffed both packs of cartridges into my bag.

"When I was a kid." Which was the truth. My dad had been an avid hunter before the accident.

For a moment, I wasn't in Dan's basement. The smell of salt water and diesel filled my nose. My eyes burned from the salt spraying my face. I was on the boat again, the water rushed up around the edges, the open ocean poured in at a rate that the bilge pump couldn't handle. Dad thrust the only life jacket at me. "Don't worry, me and your brother can swim." Except they couldn't, not in the ocean as it thrashed at them. The water took my brother, Carter, first. Then Dad. His eyes had met mine as he slipped down. His hand reached for me, a piece of wood slammed into my head and I blacked out until rescuers pulled me onto their boat.

A hand clutched my upper arm and I jerked away.

"What the hell is wrong with you?" Dan snapped. His eyes raked over me, narrowing.

"Flashback." I wiped a hand over my face. "Sorry."

He grunted, but the suspicion in his eyes did not fade. Well, that didn't matter. I wasn't going to be his friend much longer. Dan shoved past me and checked a peephole in the door.

"Bob is gone. Get out."

Well, that was short and not so sweet. I moved to the door and then paused on the threshold.

"If something happens to me, will you look out for my wife?"

I didn't think Dan's eyes could narrow further but they did. "You mean like you turn into a Nevermore?"

I didn't look away. "I mean like I get killed by a Nevermore. Or that stupid damn bear you've turned into a pet. Or any other idiot with a gun who thinks they can do what they want now that the world has ended."

Slowly Dan nodded. "If something happens to you . . . I'll see about your wife. No promises. I ain't putting my life on the line for her. But if she shows up on my doorstep, I won't turn her away."

His words were better than nothing.

I saluted him with the gun, touching the barrel to my forehead. I opened the door and stepped out. He slammed it closed behind me.

"Mighty neighborly of you. Mighty neighborly," I muttered as I headed down his driveway. At the bottom, I paused and loaded the gun, and made sure I had the safety off. If I was surprised, I had no doubt I'd forget where the dang lever rested.

I made my way along the edge of the road that led to a section of houses that were closer together. I could scavenge quicker that way. Maybe even put together some stashes for Mara if there was too much for me to carry.

The first house was empty of people. I scoured the cupboards, found a few cans of food, but nothing substantial. I shoved them into my bag and made my way into the bathroom. A few bandages, peroxide, and—

"Jackpot." I grabbed the large bottle of antihistamines. Beside it was a bottle of pain killers and even some sort of antibiotics. I read the label. It looked to be something along the lines of penicillin. Even better. They went into the bag and I ransacked the rest of the house.

Clothes, shoes, things that wouldn't go bad and wouldn't disappear fast. I grabbed a piece of paper and did a quick note of the house number and what was left in it. Pleased, I headed into the kitchen as a flow of images washed over me. I clamped down on my own thoughts and let the Nevermores images light my brain up.

Hungry. Where are those two legs?

Through this way. Four of them.

Hurry, they're getting away.

I kept myself pinned to the wall as the image words faded. I 'saw' them running after four men, all with guns.

I didn't know who to root for.

The humans.

Or the Nevermores. That thought alone should have shocked me, but the thing was, I'd seen inside their heads. Though there didn't seem to be memories of their past, the Nevermores were not mindless eating machines as we'd first thought. If anything, the more I saw, the more complicated their thoughts and processing seemed to be.

Almost as if they were evolving with each passing day. That or I was devolving. I snorted and let myself out of the house.

Checking the area between where I was and the next house first to make sure it was clear, I bolted across the lawns. The second house was not much better than the first. I took a few things, and wrote down what I left behind along with the address.

I managed to get through most of the houses before dark began to fall. The final house on the street was a bit of a monster. Three stories high, it towered over the other houses. It also looked like it would have the best view of the ocean. I shuddered.

"First floor it is." I let myself in. No need to search first, I could do that in the morning and for the first time in weeks, I was actually tired. Exhaustion crashed over me so hard that as I slumped into the first bed I found, I thought, perhaps this was it. Perhaps I was turning.

I struggled against the darkness as I fell, but it was no use.

When I opened my eyes, I was on a beach, and Mara was with me. Laughing, smiling. Healthy and unafraid. But I had to leave her and as she shouted after me, my heart broke. It was for the best. I knew it even though it was like tearing a piece of my own heart out to walk away.

She'd always been too good for me, and I'd known how lucky I was when she said yes. When she fell in love with me.

My feet dragged in the wet, warm sand, and Mara's

voice faded behind me somewhere, catching on a sob. The sand turned to dirt and I stood in a thick forest. Nevermores crept around me, their eyes full of fear.

Their hands were outstretched, as they pleaded and begged.

"Save us, he's killing us."

"You are meant to be our Alpha."

"Please."

"Please."

"PLEASE!"

The word rocketed through me and I shot upright, and clutched the gun. That last . . . it had actually happened. I was sure of it. The words seemed to hover in the night air. I stood and crept through the house. The sound of sobbing and a woman's voice begging for him to stop.

I moved quickly up the stairs, the smell of sex and blood growing with each step.

They were on the third floor. His back was to me, showing off his bare ass and his pants around his ankles. Her legs flailed as she fought to push him off.

"That's right, fight me. I like it." He laughed at her.

I lifted the gun and slammed the butt of it into the back of his head. He fell sideways off her.

With a quick spin, I brought the gun around and pointed it at him. "If I shoot him now, the Nevermores will be here fast."

I needn't have worried. She slid off the bed, grabbed a knife, and cut his throat before I'd finished speaking.

Shaking, she looked up at me. I would guess she

was in her forties, though in the dim light it was a bit hard to tell. Her dirty blonde hair was tangled up in knots and her blue eyes were wild. "You going to try the same thing?"

I shook my head. "No. I have a wife."

Her eyelids fluttered. "Let me go."

"I'm not stopping you," I pointed out.

She whipped her knife up and waved it back and forth. "You're in the doorway."

I moved so I was farther into the room, albeit on the other side of the bed from her. She grabbed her clothes and a small bag and bolted from the room. The sound of her feet on the porch and then the whisper of a Nevermore close to the house came to me.

"Shit."

I raced after her, not bothering to be quiet.

Out the door, I found her quickly, facing two female Nevermores. The woman I'd saved had her knife out, but the two Nevermores circled her.

"Stop!" I yelled the word and both Nevermore's stared at me, their jaws dropping open. I sent them both an image of running back into the bush and leaving the woman to me. They bolted.

I knew without checking that they weren't part of the pack that was close to the farm.

Double shit. Now they would tell their alpha. What kind of trouble was I bringing on myself? Too much. Too much trouble for the time I had left.

"How . . . how did you do that?" The woman stared at me, and then her mouth dropped open, too, and her eyes widened further. "You're one of them, aren't you?"

"Not yet." My shoulder's slumped. "I suggest you find somewhere inside to stay for the rest of the night."

"Why did you save me?"

So soon? Were people so cynical already?

"My wife. I would hope someone would help her if she were in a ... similar situation."

"Situation?" She started to laugh. "Is that what you call this?"

Still laughing she spun and ran down the road toward the houses I'd already searched.

I went back to the big three-story house. Wasn't like I was going to be able to sleep after this, so I might as well search the place and make good use of the time I had left.

However long that might be.

CHAPTER TWENTY - FOUR

Mara

Four men. Four men were going to ransack my house with me in it. What felt like an eternity, yet probably only ten seconds, passed as I tried to come up with a plan of how to deal with them.

"Thought you said there were people here," a gravelly voice snarled.

The man's voice startled me and I nearly popped up and waved at what I realized with great relief were humans, not Nevermores. A tingle in my stomach held me to the ground though, waiting, Nero and Missy both let out low growls. I clamped my hand over his nose and tightened my arm around her neck.

"Shhh," I whispered. "Quiet."

There was a bit of silence and then the doorknob rattled. Thank God, I'd locked it.

"I saw the bitch in my binoculars. She's here

somewhere. The big guy left this morning." A second man with a deeper tone spoke.

"Come on, let's get inside. That Nevermore at the front gate is staring at me. He's creeping the bejeesus out of me."

"Fine you pansy, in we go."

I slithered along the floor and crawled around the side of the couch and then behind it. Though not perfect, the gap was just large enough for me to fit with Nero in beside me and Missy pressed up against me. Remarkably, they were both quiet.

As I slid into my hiding place, the front door thumped once, the wood splintering. Missy lifted her lips, but no growl came out. I rubbed her head with one hand. If we were quiet, maybe we could slip out once the men were in the house and searching for me.

For me. I could imagine all too easily just why they were waiting for Bastian to leave the farm.

"Honey, I'm home!" the gravelly voiced one yelled.

They all laughed at that and I tightened my hold on the blade. I was trapped. As soon as they started looking, I had no doubt they'd find me. A sudden thought hit me. At least if it had been Nevermores breaking in, they would have just killed me. I wasn't fooling myself about what these men were after and what I would face if they found me.

Footsteps drew closer and I tensed. A body flopped onto the couch and the rank smell of sweat and blood assaulted my nose.

Nero started to growl, his wicked sharp puppy

teeth showing under a curled up lip. I put my hand over his nose again and he quieted. Missy stood slowly, the hackles along her back rising into a ridged line. But she was quiet. Waiting.

"Marty, go see if there's any food in the joint—and make it snappy. I'm famished. Denver, you go upstairs and find us our lady friend, and remember, I get first dibs." That was the one with the deeper voice on the couch.

Footsteps and grumbles receded and the leader leaned back so his head rested on the well-padded cushions of the couch. He let out a fart, a belch, and then another fart, settling himself deeper into his seat. I pinched my nose, the smell was worse than the pig farm I'd visited last year. I held my breath, and then resorted to breathing through my T-shirt 'til the worst of it passed.

"Hurry up, boys, I'm getting mighty hungry for dinner and desert. Luscious sweet, sweet pie." He laughed and I slid into a crouch, as an idea came to me. I might have a chance if I could catch them off guard. If Scout was still at the gate like they said . . . maybe I could use him too. The plan continued to form. I would have to act fast and use the element of surprise if it was going to work.

I stared up at the longish stringy hair hanging over the back of the couch. Before I thought better of it, I stood and grabbed a handful of the greasy mop at the same time as I placed the blade of my knife against the leader's neck.

"I wouldn't move or say a word unless I tell you. Got it?" I whispered at him. My adrenaline pumped hard and my nerves jangled like a trip wire.

He swallowed and his Adam's Apple bobbed against the knife.

"Very slowly get up. Nothing tricky or I'll slit your throat." I leaned forward at the same time he did. I crawled over the back of the couch without losing my grip on him or the knife. I had no intention of actually cutting him. I just wanted to get him close enough to the gate for Scout to grab him. After that, well, it was going to be dicey, but I thought it would work. It would get me outside and help the odds against me. My only thought was after I got rid of him, Missy, Nero and I could hide in the field. Or maybe head up the back trail to Dan's.

"Hey, boss, found some food . . . son of a bitch!" The one I surmised was Marty stood in the doorway between the kitchen and the living room, his hands full of our canned food, and his mouth hanging open.

"Don't just stand there, do something!" Leader Boy said.

I yanked his hair, pulling him back towards the front door, glancing around for the dogs. They were right at my feet, heeling nicely. Missy, though, was treating the men as though they were Nevermores. Now that we were out from our hiding place, she let a long growl rumble past her teeth.

I forced a laugh at him. "I have a knife to your throat, if you haven't noticed. Maybe you shouldn't be telling your friends to do anything right now."

Marty dropped the canned food and it rolled over the floor. Maybe he'd slip on it. "What do you want me to do, lady?" he growled.

"Good question," I had to think fast. "Follow us outside, nice and slow like."

More footsteps and Denver joined his buddies. I shook my head at him as he reached for his belt and what I assumed was a weapon. "Don't," I said.

He dropped his hand and I tightened mine on the knife handle.

I inched us out the door backward, drunk on adrenaline. That's my only excuse for forgetting about the fourth man.

Something hit me from behind square in the middle of my shoulders and upper back. But his blow didn't make me let go; quite the opposite.

I instinctively tightened my grip, but as I stumbled backward, the blade in my hand pulled through the leader's neck with a clean slice. His breath and blood spurted out in a low gurgle.

I wobbled a few feet away, the stunned silence from the other men giving me only a split second to make my next move. No doubt, the men still standing couldn't believe what had happened anymore than I could, and it took them a moment to recover. It was the chance I needed.

I spun and ran, blade still in my hands. Nero and Missy beside me. I pointed at them and then to the side of the gate. "STAY!"

Missy whined but herded Nero to the side.

"Get her!" I don't know which one of the men

yelled it, and it didn't matter. Not with what happened next.

I bolted to the gate where Scout crouched in the shadows off to one side. His eyes glittered as he watched me sprint toward him. The three men remaining closed in on me, fingertips brushing the back of my shirt as I panted for air, hoping for enough oxygen to make the desperate jump and climb over the metal gate.

The gate was cold and I struggled to get my hands, one still gripping the knife, on it. The bunches of metal grapes and leaves meant to be decoration bit into my skin. I managed to get half way over before the closest man grabbed my ankle.

I screamed and Missy shot out from the shadows. Snarling and growling, she launched at the man and knocked him to the ground. I pulled hard and tumbled to the ground on the other side of the fence and knocked the wind out of myself. Even with that, I made myself get to my feet and jog to the center of the road.

Missy was on the throat of the man who'd grabbed me and his hands feebly tried to fend her off. They turned to her. No, I couldn't let them hurt her.

"You think you're tough enough to take me now?" I taunted them and it worked. They left their fallen comrade on the ground and climbed the fence.

The two men followed me, cocky, and swaggering as if they knew something I didn't.

But they had their backs to Scout. I could still see

him and I gave him a slow nod. His eyes widened and a grin spread across his face. With a blur of speed, he hamstrung one of the men with his bare teeth before he knew what hit him. That one fell screaming, the sound echoing around us. It wouldn't be long before the pack showed up for this banquet. The second man half-turned to see what had happened and I rushed him. Before I made it to him, though, Scout took him down with an eerie speed. The Nevermore snapped the man's neck in one clean twist. I watched the man fall, the look of stunned surprise forever written on his face.

Marty, the one who'd been hamstrung rolled on the ground, "You stupid bitch!" he screamed as Scout jumped on his chest.

Before I could say anything, Scout ripped at Marty's neck with his hooked fingers. Blood spurted in a spray like a fountain.

I gagged at the smell and the sight and forced myself to unfreeze my legs and move. I was horrified by what I'd done, essentially leading the men into the lion's den. A lion's den I still stood in.

My semi-paralysis broke and I jogged to the gate, deliberately not looking at what Scout was doing as he sniffed around the still twitching bodies of the one man.

I put my hands on the cold metal piping that made up the gate and pulled myself up and over.

As I climbed to my side, I turned to see the pack emerge from the bush around us.

Missy whined softly, her pale cream muzzle dark with blood. "Good girl," I whispered, dropping to wrap my arms around her neck. She'd saved me.

I stood and grabbed the foot of the man Missy had taken down. I dragged him close enough to the gate so that the Nevermores could grab him.

Except he wasn't dead.

"Help me," he gurgled through the tears in his throat.

I stepped back. "No. If this is what is left of the world, it deserves the Nevermores."

I walked slowly back to the house, the screams of the last man only lasting a brief moment before they cut off.

It was not a moment I was proud of. Deep within I was horrified that I could kill four men and feel nothing. No, that wasn't true. I didn't *want* to do it, but the world was now literally dog-eat-dog, and I would go down fighting every time. Maybe I'd be upset later. Right at that moment, though, I felt a strange disconnect from my body. Something in my head said it was a form of shock.

Fine by me.

I climbed the steps to the house and stared at the leader's body on the porch. Blood pooled around him and slipped through the cracks to the ground below. His neck was cut so deeply, I could see flickers of spine.

I lost it.

Shakes started deep within my belly and spread throughout my entire body, forcing me to the ground.

I sat and leaned against the house with the body beside me as I waited for the shock to pass. When I was sure I wasn't going to throw up or faint, I made myself look around. Missy and Nero sat in front of me, a perfect pair.

"Good dogs," I said. Missy didn't sniff the body, but Nero got inquisitive. I reprimanded him lightly. "Leave it."

For a moment, I thought about the amount of meat on the man's body, that it could be good dog food. But my stomach rolled with the thought of cutting him up and trying to preserve him. I heaved silently and looked away. Yeah, that wasn't going to happen.

I stood slowly and with my hand against the house for support I leaned over the leader.

"I can't let Sebastian see me like this. I can't let him see this."

If he knew how close it had been, that there were men raiding our area already, it would only add to his stress. What if that pushed him over the edge and he turned faster than he would have otherwise? I couldn't let that happen.

Bracing myself for what I was about to do, I bent and picked up the man's feet. I dragged him off the porch and toward the gate. It was hard work, the body was floppy, heavy, and uncooperative, and by the time I made it to the halfway mark I was covered in sweat. I paused and caught my breath, and stared down at the body at my feet, really seeing it, the open gash across the neck, the surprised expression on his face.

Emotions welled up, threatening to break through the weak dam I'd build. I pushed them down. There was a place for that, but not right then. Maybe not ever again.

With a heave, I started to drag the body again, this time getting it all the way to the gate. The man I'd left on this side was gone except for a pool of blood and a single shoe that was now caught in the bars of the gate.

A grunt brought my attention to Scout, crouched back in the shadows. He stood slowly and approached me, his hands outstretched. We were going to have to work together if we were going to get this body over to him. The rest of the Nevermores were already gone. Taken their food and run.

I lifted the feet of the dead man up as high as I could. My breath came in pants and grunts. I tried not to think about Scout making a grab for me while my hands were otherwise occupied. Scout reached over the fence and grabbed one boot of the dead man, then the other. With a powerful yank he snapped the body through the air and onto his side.

With another grunt and a smile, he dragged the body behind him to the edge of the bush to his usual spot.

He did a quick glance around as if checking to make sure no one was watching, and then started in on it. His back was hunched over the dead man's chest, and a loud crunching rolled over me followed by a wet ripping sound like . . . well, I had nothing to compare it to. So it sounded like flesh being torn.

I made myself watch as he feasted on the body. Not out of desire to see what was happening. More like punishment for what I'd done. My thoughts circled around to Sebastian. How soon would it be him eating whatever he could get his hands on?

Was he okay out there, outside the fence? Was he hurt, or sleeping somewhere safe?

Would I have to see him shift and turn into a mindless eating machine, see him become like Scout, or Jessica, or the Alpha?

Which would be worse, to lose him now to the world out there beyond the fence and not know what happened, or lose him to the drug and forever have that image of Sebastian as a monster engrained in my mind?

CHAPTER
TWENTY - FIVE

Sebastian

I ran all the way home. The change was coming. I didn't have much time. My body ached to run with the others. To live wild.

But I had to make sure Mara was safe first.

Mara. Mara was the only thought I had as I raced against the ticking clock that resided in my body. One last thing I could do for her. Take her the gun and the last few items I had found. Not much of a final parting gift, but it would help her. It would even the odds for her survival.

It was the only hope I had left in me.

CHAPTER
TWENTY - SIX

Mara

spent the better part of the morning cleaning up the blood and hiding all evidence that the raiding party had ever been here. I didn't need it as a reminder of what I'd done. Or of what had almost happened. The only thing I couldn't repair was the broken door. There would be no way to explain that away.

Exhausted from the long night and hard work of lugging dead bodies around, I fell asleep on our bed around noon. Nero and Missy had once more taken up their places, curling tightly to me. Giving me their warmth and comfort.

It was a heavy sleep, dreamless and surprisingly restful. A light touch on my cheek snapped me awake and I lashed out, reaching for the knife under the pillow before I even opened my eyes. Missy let out a growl, but didn't bark.

"Easy, babe, it's me," Sebastian said.

I gasped and let go of the blade and threw myself into his arms. All my thoughts of not telling him what happened broke under his presence and the words tumbled out of me along with the tears that I hadn't been able to shed for the men I'd killed. And for the part of me that died along with them.

Sebastian stroked my hair and let me confess to him without a single word. Gulping back a final sob, I looked up and had to force myself not to react. His skin had changed in the short time he'd been gone and the patterning under the skin up his neck looked a great deal like a faint tattoo. Exactly as Jessica's had right before she left us.

"There's nothing I can say that will make this better for you, babe. But you did the right thing. You have to survive, no matter what that means, no matter who you have to kill," Sebastian continued to stroke my hair, never breaking eye contact with me. "You've got to be strong now. There's no guarantee that more raiders won't come, that you won't be attacked again. It was smart to use Scout. Really smart. In the past, there was always someone to call for help, the police or neighbors. We have to take care of each other now, whatever that means and whatever that takes."

"It scared me how little I felt for them," I whispered. "Like their deaths didn't matter when I knew they should have meant something. They had lives before too. And I just took them."

Sebastian frowned and shook his head. "Babe,

you are going to have to fight to make it through this. Don't let your fear stop you from surviving. I think it's just your way of not losing your mind. Bad shit is going to happen. There's nothing you can do about it but be strong."

He pulled me tightly into his arms and held me close. I let out a sigh of relief. "I was scared you would think I was an awful person for what I did."

"I'm probably going to try to eat people soon. I don't think you have to worry about what I think," he said. I knew he was trying to lighten the mood, but he failed miserably, the shadows of what came for him lay heavy on us, a physical weight we both tried to ignore but couldn't. I saw an image of Scout in my mind eating the body and it morphed into Sebastian, feral and nasty. My stomach rolled.

Sebastian stood. "Come on, let me show you what I found."

I followed him downstairs, prepared to be dazzled. Boy, was I disappointed. The kitchen table was covered, but most of it wasn't food. There were a number of different drugs; he'd found me allergy medicine, a few antibiotics, batteries, and canned food of miscellaneous types. Nothing that would last much more than a week or two if I really stretched it.

I forced a smile. "Looks good, how far did you have to go for all this?"

"All the way down to the north end of Bowser. Most of the homes have been ransacked, and I was chased by a few smaller packs, but it was quiet for the most part." He held out a piece of paper. "Here's what I left in the houses and the addresses. Mostly clothes, shoes, stuff like that."

I took it and looked at it. There was a smudge of blood on the corner of the paper. But Sebastian didn't have a single mark on him.

"What about Dan's? Why didn't you go there?" I brushed my fingers across the package of batteries, wishing they were edible.

He nodded and pointed to the kitchen counter. "A gun and some ammo. Better than nothing. It's loaded and the safety is off." He was sweating as he walked over to the weapon. He showed it to me and quickly went over how to load and unload it. How to hold it. How to press it into my shoulder so I didn't get a bad kickback.

He grimaced and took a step back.

Fear sliced through me. "Bastian?"

He shook his head.

A grimace crossed his face, twisting it into a parody of the man I loved. I reached out and he pushed my hand away, stumbling toward the front door.

"Bastian, no. Not yet."

He didn't turn around, just kept walking, using the furniture for support. I followed, knowing what was about to happen, wishing there was some way, wishing I could help him. Wishing I could take his place. I let out a sob; it should have been me. I should have been the one to turn, not Sebastian.

He turned at the door as his pupils shifted and slid into the vertical slit that was far too familiar to me.

Tears dripped off his chin, the last tears he would cry as a human.

"I love you." The words were garbled like he couldn't get them to spill from his lips.

I caught up to him on the porch, and he tried to push me away. I wouldn't let him go that easily. I pulled his head to mine and pressing my lips to his. Our tears sealed what would be our last kiss.

"Always, Bastian, you will always be my love. Forever," I whispered against his mouth.

"Always," he mumbled back, then jerked himself away from me and ran for the gate. He climbed over it but his movements were jerky and clumsy. As his feet touched the other side, he let out a roar, guttural and wild.

I slid to my knees where I'd killed the man the night before. Tears streamed down my face. The pack emerged from the bush, Scout creeping forward first, then the Alpha and Jessica at the back like always.

They milled around him, sniffing and grunting and he pushed them away easily, making them keep their distance. When one male got too close, Sebastian snapped his foot forward and caught it in the mouth which sent it flying backward.

I waited for the Alpha to come at Sebastian, but he didn't. Why?

Jessica had her hand on the blond Alpha, soothing him by the looks of things.

The rest of the pack gave Sebastian the distance he wanted. The pack turned as a unit and slipped back into the bush.

Sebastian stayed, standing in front of the gate like a sentinel.

He turned his head and looked back at me, his now-foreign eyes meeting mine. With a low moan, he dropped to the ground, and tucked himself into the shadows that Scout had previously occupied. With my own moan my head dropped forward 'til it touched the wooden railing.

Sebastian wasn't going with the pack. He was staying to guard me. I didn't know which would be worse; having him gone completely and knowing he had no memory left of his life before, or knowing he was trapped inside a body with unnatural desires, still remembering me and our love.

CHAPTER
TWENTY - SEVEN

Sebastian

The shadows of the gate were my home now. I wanted to run with the others, to feel the connection to the pack like that day in the field with Jessica. But there were stronger ties here. Ties to the woman in the house. Behind the fence.

She was important.

I didn't like the growling dogs. They looked like they would taste good. My belly rumbled and I held perfectly still. A bird landed on a branch above me. With a burst of speed, I shot up into the air and grabbed it, clapping it between my hands. Two bites and it was gone, feathers, bones, everything.

The hunger did not abate.

Scout came to see me twice.

Why are you not with us? We were waiting for you. We must go now. The images were of the pack restless and anxious to move to an area where more food waited. The city. They wanted to move to the cities.

I must stay. Simple. I didn't know why except the thought of leaving the women was as painful as the hunger in my gut. So I would stay. They could go. I turned my back on him.

I would stay.

Always.

But the woman didn't come out. That was wrong. Something was wrong. I would have to convince her to come out. I needed to see her.

But how?

CHAPTER TWENTY - EIGHT

$\mathcal{M}ara$

Depression is a nasty bitch, and she made herself known to me in full force.

I spent the better part of the next three days hiding inside. I slept a lot and when I was awake I wished I had the strength to take my own life. I only got up when Nero or Missy whined for food or to go out.

I dreamed of blood and death and knives, of Sebastian making love to me, of a child we never had, of the men who broke into our house, and of Jessica with her sweet smile. The dreams left me moaning and tossing, my own cries waking me only to let the sadness swallow me down again. There was no Sebastian to pull me out of my stupor and a part of me knew it was only a matter of time before I faded. Even realizing that wasn't enough. Even knowing that Nero and Missy would die along with me wasn't enough.

On the third day, a rock banged on my bedroom window and I leapt out of bed, half-dressed and completely confused. I scrambled for a weapon and came up with a knife I'd placed beside the bed.

Missy was on full alert, her hackles high and a low growl rumbling past her lips. Nero buried himself deeper into the covers.

"What the hell?" I made my way to the window and peered outside. Sebastian stood at the gate, a rock in his hand, arm cocked back and ready to throw.

I lifted the window and hung my upper body out over the edge. "Okay! I'm up, stop throwing rocks, you nut," I shouted at him. He blew a raspberry my way which I could hear even from that distance. He sat down in the cover of the bush, disappearing from view. But he was still there, he hadn't left me, not completely, and he still had some of himself left, enough to still care about me.

I forced myself to move. To get going.

Cold water makes a good bracer to wake up in the morning, and I scrubbed my body clean in the back yard with a bar of soap and two buckets of water. I even found the energy to play with the dogs, splashing them with water as they ran around the yard. Clean clothes were next on the list, and I felt more awake and ready to face whatever this day would bring me.

Sebastian was here. I could do this. He wasn't gone.

Suddenly ravenous, I went to the kitchen and pulled out a can of beans. I cracked it open and ate the whole thing down without a breath. A can of peaches was next, followed by a jar of maraschino cherries. The sweetness of the cherries slowed me down, and I took my time to savor the thick juice they were in, licking every finger to get the most out of the jar. I looked at what I'd done when I had finished, and even though I knew it was no more than I would have eaten had I been awake the last few days, I still felt stupid for eating so much in one sitting.

"Damn," I muttered for no particular reason except to say something, to break the silence. I put away the supplies Sebastian had brought home, organizing the quickly diminishing stocks. There wasn't much here, and soon, I'd be the one heading out of the property to get food stuffs.

The next few days went like the last few weeks had: draw up water, take care of the garden, check the fence, split wood, wash some clothes and hope they last a while yet, and of course, keep an eye on the gate. Through every chore, every necessary task, I wondered what the hell I was going to do with the next fifty years of my life alone on a farm surrounded by a pack of wild humans with nothing more than a pair of yellow Labradors for company. I did my best not to think about the fact they wouldn't last that entire time.

More than a week passed, maybe even longer since Sebastian had left me, and I found myself talking to the dogs, having full conversations with them. They would cock their heads and listen intently. Nero's pink tongue would hang out as he stared up at me. Missy would wink now and then.

It was in the middle of one of these conversations when our five acres suddenly felt terribly claustrophobic, so much so that I started to tremble.

I scanned the back property for where Dan had gone into the bush. A spring of hope whispered through me. Of course, Dan was still alive! He had a freaking bunker full of guns and food, the dogs and I could go to see him. Maybe even get some food. My rational self tried to remind me that Sebastian had gone to Dan's and come away with nothing but a gun. That I had convinced Sebastian not to go to Dan's, and that I didn't trust him—but my need to see and speak to another person was driving me beyond what was rational.

"Do you want to go for a walk?" I asked the dogs. Nero gave me what I chose to believe was an affirmative yip and Missy bounced around my feet.

The trek would require me to put my life on the line to reach a man I barely knew and wasn't entirely sure of, yet I was ready to do it if it meant having someone to talk to, even for a just a little while. I justified my idea with the thought that I would be able to get food from him and maybe even a second weapon, if he held true to his word.

"It's all I've got," I said.

I went inside, and grabbed the three empty knapsacks tucking them inside one another 'til there was only the one for me to carry. I couldn't take them all full, but it was a nice thought to think I would soon be filling them.

I stared at the gun. A shot would bring the

Nevermores running. I brushed a hand over it. Maybe it would be better to just take my knife.

"If we take the gun and have to use it, we'll bring the whole pack down on us." I pushed the gun away from me on the table. "And if I don't need it, it adds to the weight I have to carry." The walk was close to forty minutes. I didn't need to make things harder on myself.

I paused in my preparations; the walk would be shorter, if I ran the whole way.

"If I just take the knife, at least, I have something. I know I can kill with it." Maybe it wasn't the right decision, but I didn't think it was a bad one either.

I put the backpack on the ground and lifted Nero into it. His head stuck out along with his tongue. I laughed at him and he gave me a doggy grin, and licked at my face once I had the pack on. He was getting bigger, but I didn't think he could walk the whole way, and I didn't want to leave him here on his own in case I didn't come back. At least out there, if something happened to me, he and Missy might have a chance at finding food and surviving.

An ungodly screech filled the air and the hairs on the back of my neck stood at attention. I ran to the front door, skidding to a stop on the threshold.

The pack was in a giant circle on the far side of the gate, screaming, hollering, and otherwise making as much noise as possible. In the center of the circle was the Alpha male and . . . I let out a low moan . . .Sebastian.

Pulling myself together, I slid off the pack, put

Nero on the ground then ran to the gate. My knife clenched firmly in my hands. What I thought I was going to do about this was anyone's guess; I sure as hell didn't know. I could go back for the gun but then . . . what if I was too slow? I wasn't sure I could even shoot the thing.

The pack ignored me. They were focused solely on the two males in the circle as they jabbed and struck at one another. I knew in my gut it was a fight for dominance, but it was hard for me to see my usually passive, nonaggressive husband with his lips curled back over his teeth and growls rumbling from his mouth.

They clashed, grappling for the upper hand, and I found myself yelling along with the pack, screaming at Sebastian to finish the Alpha off. Missy barked and jumping at the fence, putting her front paws on it as if she wanted to see what was going on too.

The energy around us swirled and grew, bringing the dogs and me into the Nevermores world for a moment. We were all swept into the fight for the stronger leader. If it was a battle to the death, there was no doubt in my mind who I wanted to win, even if Sebastian was no longer himself.

I prepped myself to climb the fence. If it looked like Bastian was going down, I would climb over and help him.

The clash of bodies caused a huge dustbowl, the dry dirt road and wind making perfect conditions for it. The two men were soon caked in a fine dusting of powdered earth. The sweat rolling down their skin, caught each particle, gluing it to them. Their bodies were now a strange shade of yellow highlights and red-brown mud, which only added to the animalistic surrealism of the scene.

I took a step back and really looked at what was going on. The pack was split, half on one side of the circle and half on the other. I had a feeling Scout would be on Sebastian's side. On the right stood Jessica's father, close to the Alpha male. I scanned the crowd and spotted Scout on the left, Jessica next to him. I frowned. Wouldn't she want to be on her mate's side? A strange squirming feeling settled in my belly. She would be, unless she saw Sebastian as the better mate for her, stronger, younger and better able to care for her and any babies she had.

"You stay away from him!" I surprised myself by yelling at her.

Her eyes shot to mine. I stared her down. Sebastian was my husband. Not hers.

A snarl lifted her lips.

I bared my teeth right back at her.

That seemed to surprise her and the other Nevermores who caught our exchange, including Scout. There was a roar from the combatants and we all turned our attention back to the fight.

I took a step back and a deep breath. What did I think was going to happen? Of course, Sebastian would take a mate. That would be his job as an Alpha.

I closed my eyes and tried to slow my ever escalating thoughts, tried to banish a sudden image of Jessica and Sebastian rolling on the ground, their bodies naked and intertwined, as they wrestled in a far different way than he was now entangled with the Alpha. He wouldn't do it. I had to believe there was enough of Sebastian left that he wouldn't have sex with Jessica. My stomach rolled and I swallowed the bile that suddenly rose in my throat. A burn of anger started in me, one that fired me up like nothing else. I'd never been a jealous wife. Apparently there was a time and a place for everything.

Sebastian hadn't even done anything and already the effects of jealousy and bitterness at the thought of Bastian and Jessica together made me want to vomit.

A crack of bone snapped my eyes open. The Alpha male was on the ground, his ankle twisted at the wrong angle. He let out a moan and dropped his head, defeated by his younger, stronger opponent. The pack swirled around, hopping and thumping the ground with their hands and feet, some of them diving into their fallen leader and taking pot shots at him.

The pack stepped back, their eager grunts and gestures making it clear even to me that they wanted Sebastian to finish him off. This was the final moment of his humanity and I knew it. The minute he killed the man helpless at his feet would be the minute I had to say goodbye to him forever. If it had been a battle to the end, that would have been different, survival, but not this killing of a defenseless creature at his feet.

Sebastian walked over to the Alpha and stared down at him, not moving, just looking. The Alpha kept his eyes down and held perfectly still. He knew as well as the rest what was coming.

"Sebastian," I said, not truly thinking he would

heed me. To my disbelief, he turned and looked me in the eye. Hope, fragile and fleeting, whispered through me. "Don't do this. Don't let them take the last of what makes you, you. You aren't a monster, love. You aren't."

My eyes filled with tears but I didn't cry. I put every emotion I could into my next words, hoping he would listen.

"Don't kill him."

The pack, perhaps sensing my interference grumbled, low and angry. They milled toward the gate and I stepped out of reach but I never broke eye contact with Sebastian.

Something flickered in those alien eyes—an emotion that was so achingly human—a piece of my husband I had feared would be gone forever.

Compassion.

He stepped away from the Alpha and growled at the pack who then froze in their advance on me and the gate. A second, lower growl and they backed off, and slunk into the bush from where they had come. All except for Jessica who hovered close by, her rail thin body swaying to music I couldn't hear, and the previous Alpha who pulled himself to his feet and dragging his broken ankle, limped down the road alone, away from the pack's territory. Jessica didn't even look at her mate as he passed her. She had eyes for only one person.

Sebastian stared at Jessica and I recognized the look, seeing as he'd given it to me more than once. His eyes were dark with desire, his lips parted and a steady pulse throbbed at the base of his neck. She preened under his gaze, a noise similar to a purr bubbling out of her as the swaying intensified, her tiny hips rocking faster and faster, side to side.

I didn't want to see this. It was bad enough knowing it would happen right outside the home Sebastian and I had started to make for ourselves. I turned my back headed for the house, feeling if I ran it would somehow made things worse. A low grumble from Sebastian and an answering purr from Jessica sped my feet up. But I didn't run. Around the back of the house I went, straight to the garden.

I stared at the ground, far enough away that I couldn't hear anything. A girlish shriek made me jump. On second thought, the back fences needed checking. Like right now.

I ran, the dogs with me, their panting giving them away. I ran to out to where the grass was the longest. To where I didn't think I could be seen and I surely couldn't see what was going on outside my fence.

Through the tall grass that would have one day been pasture for the pony I'd hoped to have for a child, past the tall maple we'd tied a rope to for a tire swing, all the way to the back fence where I collapsed to my knees.

Breathing hard, my blood thumped in my ears. I strained to hear noises from Sebastian and Jessica while at the same time desperately praying I wouldn't. My blood slowed, and my heart rate settling back to a steady beat. There was nothing but the birds in the trees and the occasional song of a frog that reached me. Nero plunked himself down beside me and rolled on his back, luxuriating in the cool grass. I wished I could be as nonchalant about life, could enjoy even the little moments.

Missy sat beside me, then laid down and put her head on her paws. Waiting for me to make a move.

"I can't do this, not on my own, not by myself." I lay on the ground and stared up at the blue sky with the tall, brilliantly green stalks of grass surrounding me. As if I was a child again. I was in a daze with my heart numb as I struggled with jealousy, anger, and pain. The three emotions warred for my attention. In the back of my mind, I had thought Sebastian would be strong enough to break through the drug's effects. He'd said he hadn't gotten a full dose after all. And then when he had stayed to watch over me, when he seemed to still remember me, I thought he would come back to himself. That hope was dashed against the reality of what was happening outside the gate.

My head knew it would be unfair to judge him; he would never have pursued Jessica if he was in his right mind. But that knowledge didn't change how I felt, or how much it hurt me to see him want her.

I closed my eyes, and when I opened them again, I knew I was dreaming, knew it wasn't real, but I wanted it to be.

Sebastian stood across the field from me, the summer season having slipped into fall and the grass golden in the fading sunlight. "What are you staring at, babe?"

I laughed and stood, my balance off kilter, and

when I looked down I realized why. I was pregnant, and not just a little bit, a lot pregnant. I ran my hands over my belly, the baby rolling under my fingertips.

"We're pregnant," I said, looking to Sebastian for confirmation of what I felt inside.

He smiled and started towards me. "Of course, we are. That's why I took the shot, remember?"

My elation faded. "No, you didn't take the shot, couldn't have. It turns people into monsters."

Sebastian laughed and then was suddenly at my side his hands on my belly. "No one turns into monsters, babe. We are the future, the others, those who didn't take the shot, they're the past." He held a mirror up to my face and I gasped.

Yellow eyes stared at me from what looked like my face, a gaunt, emaciated version of my face with jaundiced skin pulled tightly over the bones. I stared at my arms as the flesh shrunk and the skin stretched showing every sinew and ligament in clear relief. Horror rippled through me, my mouth dry. I clung to my disbelief like a life raft in rough seas.

"No. I can't take the shot, I can't. I'm too allergic!" I backed away from Sebastian. He didn't change, didn't look any different and then he smiled, a big toothy grin that showed me row upon row of shark teeth glinting down on me. He lunged and I gasped as I sat bolt upright in the long grass, my hand going to my stomach.

CHAPTER TWENTY - NINE

Sebastian

The female in front of me squealed and laughed as my hand slid over her arm. I jerked back as though I'd been burned.

No. I didn't want her. I turned and watched the woman behind the fence hurry away. Her back was stiff, every muscle in her body told me a story. Hurt, she was hurt and trying to hide it. Like always.

The female grabbed me between the legs and I let out an involuntary groan before I pushed her off me.

Why do you stare after her? She cannot be with us. It is not safe for her. You could not protect her.

I glanced at the female, a name floating around in my brain. Jessica. Her name was Jessica. She reeled back as if I slapped her.

Not my name. No longer her. Stronger. I am Fire now.

I raised both eyebrows. New names?

Why will you not mind speak with me?

I didn't know exactly why, except that it had to do with the other woman. The one who was hurt. The one who meant something to me. I let Fire lead me away, let her draw me into the bush where the remainder of the pack waited.

The male who smelled like Fire, the one whose blood was the same grabbed her and pulled her from my side. Her eyes shot to mine and a faint memory tickled.

"I'll take care of you. When the time comes and I . . . when I turn. I'll take care of you. I won't let him hurt you ever again."

Her arms wrapped around me, every pretense of the hard and wanton young woman gone in a flood of tears and soft sobs. "Why?"

"Because I don't think you're really all that bad."

I shook my head. Her father hurt her. Took her body. She stood beside him but she was smaller and the pack looked to me now. If I let him take her, I would no longer be Alpha. But if I took her, then she would be my mate.

Let her go. I sent the image as strongly as I was able. The pack around me shook and several stepped back.

Fire's father grinned and shook his head.

She is mine. You have a mate. I smell it on you. You have no desire for this one.

It didn't matter that he was right. I'd made a promise to her, what seemed like a long time ago. And

I knew I had to keep it or lose something important. Like listening to the woman behind the fence speak. Don't do it. That was what she'd said.

But she wasn't here to stop me this time.

I leapt forward and grabbed Fire, throwing her away from him. He snarled up at me and began to bow his head in submission. I didn't want submission. I saw only one way out. I grabbed him around the throat and lifted him above my head. He snarled and kicked, clawed at my arms, but I held him there as the breath in his body faded and his heart gave out. When he went limp and I was sure he was dead, I tossed his body to the side.

The others could eat him. I would not. I could not.

I made my way through the thick bush to the spot by the gate. I crouched and waited. I wanted to hear the woman's voice again.

I wanted to be near her.

There was a promise to her that whispered through my mind that I could not let go of.

Always.

Acknowledgements

The first version of Sundered was released five years ago. The story still resonated with me, and many, many readers, so I thought it was time it had a refresher now that I have a bit better skill in the craft of writing. And to be totally honest, Sebastian's side of the story needed to be told, too. To see inside his head and understand what he went through.

Thank you to those who encouraged me to dive back into the world of Nevermore. You know who you are. To the fans who have continued to ask me what is happening in this particular world, I hope you will not be disappointed with the additions and depth I was able to bring to this series. Many thanks as always go to my amazing team. Editors: Tina Winograd, Stephanie Erickson, and Shannon Page. And many thanks to my early readers for their hawk eyes on the typos.

I have been blessed to be surrounded with people who help take my work to a higher level each time I work on a book. Thank you!

AUTHORS NOTE

Thanks for reading "Sundered". I truly hope you enjoyed the beginning of Mara and Sebastian's story, and the world I've created for them. If you loved this book, one of the best things you can do is leave a review for it. Most of my books are available across all platforms, so feel free to spread the word.

Again, thank you for coming on this ride with me, I hope we'll take many more together. The rest of The Nevermore Trilogy, along with most of my other novels, are available in both ebook and paperback format on all major retailers. You will find purchase links on my website at:

www.shannonmayer.com

Enjoy!

ABOUT THE AUTHOR

Shannon Mayer lives in the southwestern tip of Canada with her husband, dog, cats, horse, and cows. When not writing she spends her time staring at immense amounts of rain, herding old people (similar to herding cats) and attempting to stay out of trouble. Especially that last is difficult for her.

She is the USA Today Bestselling author of the The Rylee Adamson Novels, The Elemental Series, The Nevermore Trilogy, The Venom Trilogy and several contemporary romances. Please visit her website for more information on her novels.

www.shannonmayer.com

Ms. Mayer's books can be found at these retailers:

Amazon   iTunes
Barnes & Noble   Smashwords
Kobo

Made in the USA
Las Vegas, NV
15 January 2021

15827647R00148